"Mallick offers an impress⁻·¹
woman caught between tr⸱
sense of empowerment."
~ *Kirkus Reviews*

D1636812

"*The Black-Marketer's Daughter* is a key-hole look at a few things: a mismatched marriage, the plight of immigrants in the U.S., the emotional toll of culture shock, and the brutal way Muslim women are treated, especially by men within their own community. Titling it—defining the heroine by her relationship to a man rather than as a woman in her own right—suggests how deeply ingrained that inequality can be."
~ *IndieReader Reviews*

"*The Black-Marketer's Daughter* is a beautifully written tale of womanly courage and love, embellished with the poetry of Omar Khayyam. Although male, Suman Mallick has written exquisitely from a woman's point of view to give us Zuleikha, a fanciful young Pakistani woman in an arranged marriage in America, and her story makes this concise, riveting book a love letter to all domestic violence victims, especially Muslim women. This finely wrought novel offers redemption and a way out from under the patriarchal religious dogma that purports to exalt women but in fact degrades the female sex. I highly recommend this book!"
~ **Sherry Jones, internationally bestselling author of *The Jewel of Medina***

"In *The Black-Marketer's Daughter*, Mallick employs careful, measured prose to convey a punishing story: that of a Muslim woman, disoriented and alone in America, who slips further and further into the gears of a society built on misogyny and self-interest. Ultimately, her strongest advocate may be the perception and empathy Mallick brings to revealing the harrowing truth of her situation."

~ **Dan DeWeese, author of *Gielgud* and *You Don't Love This Man***

"*The Black-Marketer's Daughter* is the portrait of a woman who endures violence, intimidation, xenophobia and grief, and yet refuses to be called a victim. In this slender novel, Suman Mallick deftly navigates the funhouse maze of immigrant life in contemporary America—around each corner the possibility of a delight, a terror, or a distorted reflection of oneself."

~ **Matthew Valentine, Winner, Montana Prize for Fiction; Lecturer, University of Texas at Austin**

"This novel reminds us that our lives spring from cultural traditions we must either escape or embrace. With rich language and a keen eye for the details of a small enclave in North Texas, Suman Mallick reveals a complex world hidden within American society."

~ **Andrew Mitin, author of *Time Spent Away***

"In *The Black-Marketer's Daughter*, Suman Mallick explores the myriad systems by which this world further entraps victims of violence—the law, the mosque, the marriage—and offers us a way through."

~ **Matthew Robinson, author of *The Horse Latitudes***

THE
BLACK-MARKETER'S
DAUGHTER

: SUMAN MALLICK :

atmosphere press

In loving memories of my father and of Joli.

Then to the rolling Heav'n itself I cried,
Asking, "What Lamp had Destiny to guide
Her little Children stumbling in the Dark?"
And—"A blind Understanding!" Heav'n replied.

~ Edward Fitzgerald,
Rubáiyát of Omar Khayyám

: PART I :

Following a traditional wedding in her hometown of Lahore, Pakistan, Zuleikha arrives in Irving, Texas with her American husband Iskander Khan, just as spring ends and the sun starts barbequing the land all day in what she'll come to decide is a typical Texas style, by overdoing it, charring it crisp. She can't help but be impressed by the earnestness with which Iskander sets off about making the two major purchases stipulated by their marriage contract. The first—after she acquires her driver's license—is a used car for her. They respond to several ads until her aesthetics intersect with Iskander's sensibilities at a navy economy sedan. Zuleikha finds the car practical and unpretentious, and the color suitably understated. The radio, however, seems to have an electrical short: the on/off and volume button has a mind all its own. But otherwise the vehicle shows few signs of wear, and the gas mileage—Iskander points out to his wife—is more than acceptable. The owners have saved records of the oil changes and other routine maintenance with as much care as some couples reserve for their children's photographs and mementos. They're relocating to Thailand. When they aren't looking, Iskander whispers to Zuleikha, "Let me do the talking." He talks the sellers into six hundred dollars less than their asking price, writes the check and signs it with a flourish, and requests a Bill of Sale and the Title.

Later, after they have driven home separately, he tells Zuleikha with a sly smile, "I'll take a look at the radio this weekend. You're just going to drive to the store and back for now, anyways, and later, when the time is right, I'll upgrade you to something bigger."

But something comes up at Iskander's work that weekend, keeping him cloistered in front of his computer, and he does not have time to look at the radio. Zuleikha does not mind; she finds a small measure of pride imagining how important her husband must be at work. Then one thing after another keeps intruding in their newlywed lives, and eventually she gets used to the quirky radio as one gets used to a colorful, peculiar aunt.

When her husband Iskander was nine, his father finally fulfilled his lifelong ambition of emigrating to the west with his family. Zuleikha learned this before the wedding, of course, but over dinner one evening, wanting to know more about this man she didn't even know existed five months ago, she asks about that immigration process.

"It only happened because Ronnie and Zia decided to become buddies," Iskander says.

"Ronnie?" she asks.

"That would be Ronald Reagan. President Ronald Reagan."

"Reagan, oh! That's the actor, right? *Love is on the air? That Hagen Girl?* He was in a lot of movies before he became President, wasn't he?"

"Some people like to think of him as the guy who ended the Cold War, the guy whose face should be carved into Mount...never mind." Iskander presses his lips into a sly smile.

In that smile Zuleikha detects the self-satisfied air of someone who's just proven—as if there was any doubt—that he knows more about the real world than the person across the table.

"I'll explain later," he says. "And maybe we can make a road trip to Mount Rushmore sometime so you can see for yourself how impressive it is. But to answer your question, since the two presidents were getting along so well, signing arms treaties, etc., I'm sure it didn't take long for some genius in the State Department to figure out there were good smart engineers like my dad out there that this country could really use."

"But not video store owners," Zuleikha nods in agreement. "That's what Papajaan always told us. It's why he got so upset when Jameel wanted to study Farsi, and not engineering, at the university."

"Well, first of all, those days are gone. There are now plenty of Pakistani video store owners right here in suburban Irving." Zuleikha's face must have again given away her surprise, because Iskander asks, "Don't believe me? I'll show you the next time we go for a drive. And not just in Irving, they're all over Dallas-Fort Worth. But did your dad also get upset when you wanted to study the piano?"

"No. My situation was different than my brother's. I was always Papajaan's favorite and he let me do what I wanted, besides, it was classical music, because he probably—he figured—"

She looks down at her plate, feeling the heat fanning across her cheeks. The *nihari* she's made for dinner gapes back at her, and now she feels further ashamed, remembering the insistence in her Mamajaan's voice: *The measurements have to be just right, Beti, and you have to grind those spices by hand, and put them in the cloth bundle like this; no, no! Not dump them like that, but gently, like this, or any husband will spit it out.*

"This stew is pretty good," Iskander says. "But movies? You think of Reagan and you think of his old movies? That's cute!"

The following weekend, Iskander points to a newspaper advertisement for a grand sale on pianos. The instrument is the second big-ticket item promised by the groom, and agreed upon and signed off by the groom's father during the marriage contract negotiations.

The air conditioner gushes in full blast as they drive up the Dallas North Tollway toward the Galleria. Outside, the dust in the air shimmers in the sun like the expansive muslin train of an extravagant wedding gown.

"I'm glad you'll have this," Iskander tells her. "I never wanted one of those *dupatta*-wearing wives who, after the cleaning and before the cooking, spend all day watching junk on TV. It's so nice that *you* have a real hobby."

Inside Cranbrook's Pianos, the saleslady, a pretty redhead named Peggy, possesses a charming smile that exposes all of her small white even teeth. She politely inquires if the Khans have a budget.

"Two thousand dollars," Iskander says. "By the way, how much is delivery?"

Peggy smiles even more sweetly and professionally than before. "A hundred and fifty," she says. "And that's a very good price point to start owning a piano. But if you don't mind, may I recommend a used one? They're better than anything new you can buy at that price, and we make sure they're perfect before they leave the store. In fact, my husband's the head technician here, and his team does great work, *plus* we provide one free tune-up later."

Zuleikha is impressed by Peggy's cool demeanor as they follow her across the main showroom and into a smaller, windowless room at the back. There the two women busy themselves trying out the various instruments, filling the constrained air with snippets of melody not unlike the sometimes listless, sometimes manic chirping of birds entrapped within an enclosure at a zoo, until Zuleikha settles on a Story & Clark Console within their price range.

"I think we have a winner," Peggy announces with a satisfied smile.

Zuleikha looks at Iskander and asks, "What do you think?"

"I'm pretty sure it'll fit in our nook lengthwise, but let's just confirm." Iskander matter-of-factly produces a black-and-yellow tape measure out of his pocket.

Zuleikha, mortified, steals a quick glance at Peggy, but finds the saleswoman unperturbed, her eyes focused complaisantly upon Iskander.

"But they're all the same length," Zuleikha says, "unless they have fewer keys, and we mustn't get one of those!"

"Did you just say *mustn't*? Is that still a word?" Iskander presses his lips into that sly smile, his trademark.

Zuleikha blushes right through to the roots of her hair.

The Story & Clark does not, however, come with its own piano bench.

"No problem," Iskander confidently declares. "We'll

just find one on Craigslist."

But finding an orphan piano bench on its own, minus the piano, turns out to be a more difficult proposition than Iskander might have imagined. They both search online for days. Iskander eventually comes across a posting and excitedly points it out to his wife. But then he groans as he expands the little map on the right to find the seller's location.

"Holy cow, that's almost all the way to Oklahoma! It'll cost more in gas to get there and back than what they want for it."

"Don't worry too much about it," Zuleikha says. "I'll manage for the time being with a dining room chair."

But her husband insists that she must have something appropriate to sit on. The dining room chair may not be good for her posture while playing piano.

"We'll find one," he tells her with a wink. "I'll keep looking. Just give me a little time."

Her piano is a delight. While its sound is neither very big nor bright, it is quite mellow and captures the full spectrum of tonal color as far as she can tell. What it lacks in terms of high harmonics, it makes up for with an understated resonance. Perhaps more importantly than anything else, the Story & Clark does not sound tinny or metallic like her old Casio keyboard.

She smiles to herself remembering her old instrument.

Zuleikha and the piano was a love story that almost did not happen. She had learned to play the harmonium as a child and was good at it; but as far as she was concerned, the harmonium was one thing, the piano another. Walking back home from school past one of the gated villas in which someone played every day, she would be enthralled by the sound. Whoever it was remained hidden from view but played beautifully and religiously every day. By that time, Zuleikha was only peripherally religious; she attended all the ceremonies and followed all the protocols, but more out of an underlying sense of belonging, duty and fear than anything else. This—the piano—she could see herself, feel herself, being a true devotee of this.

"If that's what you really, really want to do, then I'll just have to find you one, Insaah'Allah," Papajaan announced.

"Where are you going to find a piano in Lahore?" Mamajaan harrumphed, serving tea. "What's it going to cost? And where, explain this to me, are we going to put it?"

Looking around the already cramped living room of their second story flat, Zuleikha knew that her mother had a valid point. Across the sofa on which she sat was the web of cracks on the wall that Jameel had nicknamed the Indus River Delta. Pushing against her back was the comforter that Mamajaan forbade her family from spreading out to comfort themselves, lest it reveal the tear on the sofa that she had stitched over. Zuleikha had only dreamed her dream for months; she had not contemplated the practical realities that had to be seen to in order to make that dream a reality.

"We'll make room. This will serve her well. And you forget that I am a well-connected man," Papajaan said. "I can find a piano for my daughter. You just see."

"I know. I know of your connections to the underworlds," Mamajaan replied, pulling back from her husband the plate of *gola* kababs and brown onions. "Save the rest for Jameel. But you didn't answer me: what's it going to cost? And how will we pay for lessons? And even if you figure all that out, where will you put a piano in this place?"

Weeks of negotiation and research followed. Papajaan made calls. In the end, he told Zuleikha that a keyboard was the best that could be done under the circumstances. Zuleikha quickly saw the wisdom in his logic. She did not argue, but she also let it be known that only a full-size instrument would do for proper training.

Still, when Papajaan finally brought the Casio home one evening, there was no triumph in his voice, nor his braggadocious smile, but only trepidation.

"I'll make you a bench and a seat for it with my own hands. That I know how to do, and you know that," he told her by way of compensating for the compromise. "You may not have exactly the piano you wanted, but you'll have the best bench and seat for your toy, you'll see."

"This is not a toy to me, Papajaan," she corrected him.

Papajaan finally smiled. "Remember how I can hammer nails with my eyes closed? Now, if you truly love this, then you, too, will be able to tame it with your eyes closed, and this will all have been worth it. Maybe, someday, you'll play me 'Ahmad's Blues.'"

She did not have the heart to tell him then that as much as she enjoyed listening to the jazz pianist who had pierced Papajaan's soul, her own interest in music lay elsewhere. Instead, she pointed to the blackened nails, the thick corns and calluses in his fingers, and said, "Please don't hammer with your eyes closed when you make the table and the bench."

A week later, Iskander relents.

"I am sick of watching you bending over that piano

that way," he tells his wife. "Let's make that drive and buy that bench before someone else gets it. We'll just take your car—it takes less gas."

"He is a very considerate man, so conscientious," she says to her mother during one of their bi-weekly, long-distance telephone calls. Hesitating, she adds, "In fact, sometimes I feel he was brought up too perfect."

"Do you hear what you are saying?" Mamajaan asks. "Do you know how much sacrifice it took, how many prayers, to find someone considerate? And with principles? Nobody is born with a conscience, you know! So now are you complaining that he was raised right?"

"I'm not complaining, Mamajaan. I'm just saying it's a little strange, that's all. And not just him, but the few friends he has—at the mosque, at work—they are all like that, smiling but never laughing, so serious all the time. We went to the movies Saturday, and he obsessed over which of the empty seats would provide the most optimal viewing, but afterwards, when I asked what he thought of the movie itself, he only responded, *interesting.*"

"So he took you to a movie, found you good seats, and you didn't like what he said afterwards about the movie?" Mamajaan asks. "Girls these days!"

Zuleikha can just picture her mother, ten hours ahead, seated on the stool by the phone, combing her shingled hair, exhausted from running the household all day, counting down the days until Jameel is married and she has a daughter-in-law to lend a helping hand. But this picture still doesn't lessen the sting of being judged by the standards of the time and place where her mother was born and bred.

"Do you know, Mamajaan, that I can't think of a single mother-daughter talk between us in all these years that I've ever wanted to make into a family myth to share with friends?"

"What are you talking about? If you are confused it's your father's fault, *Beti*—not mine—for letting you do whatever you wanted, getting into all that mischief," Mamajaan laments.

Fall in Texas. The sun reclines in the western sky, bathing Fair Park in an incandescent orange glow. At the State Fair, Zuleikha inhales the intense aromas of fried food everywhere, and exhales the first sighs of mercy from the just-ended summer heat. She wears a designer *Shalwar Kameez* with hand-stitched embroidery, the *dupatta* casually draped over her shoulders and pinned in place, a simple necklace and pair of earrings to complement the intricate design of her outfit. Strolling with her husband, she feels extravagant and impulsive, her mood like an accessory. Eyes linger upon her face, her dress, her body. The sense of being stared at fills her with excitement. She wipes powdered sugar from Belgian waffles off her husband's chin and wants to ride the giant Ferris wheel.

As they approach it, the crowd becomes dense, nearly impassable. She cranes her neck to peer above the ant crawl of people, her face flush.

Iskander disappears to check on the wait time. "It'll be forty-five minutes to an hour," he says when he returns. They both glance at their watches. "But you know what? I've never been up there either," Iskander continues. "Let's do this thing!"

Zuleikha scans her husband's face. "Are you sure? We don't have to—"

"Don't be silly." Instead of his usual smile, he laughs. He has a rich, warm laugh. "We're in no rush. Or are you having second thoughts now that you see how high it is?"

"No. Yes. Ok then."

They wait in line behind a lanky man with two children. "What time is it?" the boy asks.

His little sister, no more than four, replies in a song-song voice, "It's time to choose."

"What time is it?"

"It's time to choose."

Their father says to no one in particular, "I think it's about time you kids stopped watching that damn show. Tell you what time it is: time for dad to have a beer."

"A beer actually sounds like a great idea," Iskander tells Zuleikha. "I know you don't like the taste, so let me surprise you with something else. I'll be right back."

He leaves her for a few minutes, comes back with his beer and a margarita in a plastic cup. The intense, salt-and-lemony taste makes Zuleikha's face pucker. The early October evening turns mercurial. The sight of the children just ahead of them in line prompts her to recall fairs from her own childhood—fairs are fun everywhere. The memories make her feel nostalgic and also a touch melancholy. She wishes she had a notebook, or better yet, a video camera to record the chatter around her, or else all she will remember when she looks back upon this evening is the boundless energy, just as all she can remember now from those fairs of her childhood are faded sensations. Fireworks light up the evening sky. It makes her want to spill a story—her story—into an open book, a turn-of-the-last-century, quixotic romance.

Eventually, they are let in a passenger capsule with the excited children and their father. The cabin door is locked behind them, the big wheel squeaks and turns, they rise up a little, the wheel stops. More passengers are let into other cabins below.

"What time is it?" big brother asks as the wheel starts turning again.

"It's time to choose."

The man smiles apologetically and speaks to Iskander with exaggerated exhaustion and feigned disgust. "Don't have kids, man; don't ever have kids. Sorry, ma'am. I'm only doing my civic duty to warn all my fellow men. To think, I traded in my custom Harley for them."

"Those Harleys are sweet," Iskander says.

"Hundred and twenty-seven inches, loud as hell. Yep, that was one bad-ass ride. Now all I've got to show for my life are these good-ass munchkins." He pulls the little girl close, tousles her hair and kisses her.

The stranger's craving for a drink in the presence of his children, his tasteless advice to her husband in her presence, has been making Zuleikha feel vaguely hostile to this man. But now she sees the expression of unabashed joy in the little girl's face and decides that this man is not that different from her own father after all, a soft interior encased by a hardened shell.

The Ferris wheel finally picks up steam. They rise up into the evening sky and a tiny shiver passes through Zuleikha. She leans closer to Iskander until she can feel the corduroy of his pants grazing against the thin fabric of her *Shalwar*.

Iskander says, "Dang, there was a time when I'd have

loved to ride one of those."

"What are you talking about?" a surprised Zuleikha asks her husband.

"Uh oh," the man snickers.

"No, no, I don't mind," she says hastily. "You used to want to ride a motorcycle?"

Iskander presses his lips and smiles. "Not wanted; did."

"Really?"

"Let's just forget I said that."

"No, I want to know. You rode a motorcycle? What kind of motorcycle?" she insists.

"Well, if you must know, I used to own a Ducati. God, it's been what, five years, maybe?" Iskander says. "I bought it, used, after I first got my job, to ride on the weekends. Feels so long ago. Follies of my youth."

"You say that as if you were an old man," Zuleikha points out. "I just have to say, that's pretty wild. You just don't look like the type of man who'd do such a thing."

"Which is probably why my parents never suspected a thing."

They crest the peak of the Ferris wheel's height, and the children clamor for their father's attention, pointing to sights, quizzing him about landmarks of the metroplex.

"What happened to it?" Zuleikha asks.

"Let's not talk about it anymore, okay?"

"But I'm your wife. Why can't you talk to me about it?"

Iskander's silence evolves into its own response. She looks away, becomes aware of the cacophony of fair sounds as their cabin completes its first revolution and reaches ground level.

She feels Iskander's arm brush her shoulder, a gentle

squeeze.

"You're right," he says. "I guess I can tell you about it. Just don't ever mention anything to anyone else, especially my parents, all right? My mom will have a heart attack over nothing."

"I'm sorry. If it brings back bad memories, you don't have to talk about it."

"I dropped it, and it wasn't my fault." As they rise back up into the night sky, the white noise of the fair recedes while Iskander stares off into the distance. "It was a Sunday afternoon and I was going to the office to do something. I had the green light and this car was supposed to yield to me, except it didn't. Pulled right in front, cut me off. I put the bike down. No! I got stuck under it and it dragged me fifty feet or so, straight through the intersection until we ended up in a ditch. I was geared up, but still lost a lot of skin. Nothing else, thank God! But the thought, the fear that I was going to die as I was careening across that road with the bike on top of my body like a wild beast—that was it for me. There's a saying: if you make it past the first drop, make it the last drop. The bike was gone after that."

"Unbelievable!" the man says, shaking his head. They both look up and Zuleikha realizes he has been eavesdropping. "What did the driver do?"

"That's the thing. There was more than one person in the car—I could see them, it was all a blur but I could tell—and they did absolutely nothing; slowed down, watched the whole thing, then just sped up and took off." Iskander raises his hand in resignation. "And before you ask if I was able to notice anything else about the car, you gotta remember I was in shock, too busy checking to make sure

I still had my limbs attached to my body to do anything else. I've never forgiven them, don't think I ever will."

"Son of a bitch!" the man exclaims, running his fingers through his sandy blonde hair. Zuleikha's eyes drift over to the children, but the children pay no attention to their father.

On their way down the second time, the boy starts again. "What time is it?"

"It's time to choose," the little girl sings.

"Well I'll tell you, Karma's gonna get 'em someday," her father announces. "And that's it, you two. No more sugar tonight, you hear me?"

"Well, if you believe that, I still have some dot-com stocks I can sell you," Iskander says with a hearty laugh. He turns to his wife. "Are you feeling okay? You look a little giddy. It must be that margarita."

"I'm more than a little shocked. It reminds me of a line from this story I read once, it was in Urdu so it's hard to translate exactly, but what it means is how the night can sometimes illuminate more than the day. Or it could be the alcohol."

Iskander squeezes her shoulder again, as if he understands her utterly.

Zuleikha feels washed over by waves, freshened and yet salty, and leans on her husband as if he's the sand on the shore.

On weekday mornings, after Iskander leaves for work, she takes a walk along the Campion Trail. Several times she exchanges smiles, then hellos, with a tallish, middle-aged, pale woman with a frank smile. They eventually introduce themselves to each other, and thus Zuleikha ends up befriending Marianne, who manages an upscale restaurant in Addison.

"If I didn't know any better," it doesn't take Marianne long to ask, "I'd say that there's something nagging you, Zuleikha. Care to share?"

"What? No, no! I'm just trying to get used to this place still." Zuleikha is momentarily taken aback by Marianne's directness so soon into their friendship. "Like the grocery store you told me about, it's so much cleaner *and* the prices are so much more reasonable, but I didn't even know it was there, you know. Things like that."

"Okay, if you say so. But I'm beginning to think you are one of those rare people who think more than they should. It must be why you walk so slow. Let's up the pace a little, okay? Unlike you, some of us—especially those that eat lunch *and* dinner at a restaurant six days a week—could stand to lose a few pounds. Not to mention the fact that I have to go home and get ready to go to work at that place."

As they walk faster, breathing briskly, the extra exertion lights up Marianne's face. She pounds the pavement with a smile, waving at everyone. After a while, she says, "I'm still not sure I believe you entirely, though."

"It's probably nothing, really," Zuleikha says, suddenly feeling despondent and homesick. "Just that sometimes I can't figure my husband out."

"Oh honey, all men are like that. You've just reached that stage in your relationship when the honeymoon's over and you've started finding out how obnoxious and weird he is."

"Obnoxious? No! Weird? Well, a little, I guess. Why can't they be like they used to be in the movies? You'd think that a man who used to ride a motorcycle would be a little more...I don't know how to explain it."

"Manly?"

"No, that's not what I mean. Lively, maybe. Or alive, or full of life—that's what I mean! I'll give you an example: it's like when I found out about his bike last fall: that was interesting to me, sure, but it was so much more than that. Exciting, fascinating, a little scary."

They reach the Royal Lane underpass and turn around. Sunlight reflects off the murky waters of the Elm Fork Trinity in shades of molten gold, as if in an impressionistic painting. The landscape imparts a forlorn feeling that is at once familiar and foreign. Past the water and a thicket of trees, colorfully attired golfers in their carts pursue a pastime that also feels abstractly alien to Zuleikha.

"But that same biker has now become someone who only says one thing when it comes to my playing the piano," she says. "*Interesting.* He never calls it melancholy, or fantastic; never uses any of the words that took me so long to get used to at the music academy: *untidy, unstable,* or the really maddening ones—*mannered, affected,* all of which I know I deserve to hear while I'm at the piano, you know?"

"Interesting," Marianne says, then laughs at her own joke.

Zuleikha smiles wryly. "That word feels to me like an eczema that won't go away, no matter what cream you put on it. I think it's some kind of defense mechanism for him: an adjective to ascribe to all things created by people without *real* jobs. Each time I hear it, I feel a ferocious loathing, and the nerves at the tips of my fingers go dead. And now I'm starting to dread going near the piano whenever Iskander's home."

"You have a complicated way of describing things sometimes, did you know that? Must be that strange English they taught in school in Pakistan. Over here, we just call it a tic. But why don't you find a *real* job and show him what you can do?"

Zuleikha retreats into silence.

"Doesn't want you to work, huh?" Marianne says as they round a bend and the entrance to the trail looms into view. "Must be nice. Here I am, thrice divorced, sometimes working six days a week to pay for my kid's college, because her dad won't spare a dime, and there you are, just three streets over. You better not tell me that he's also great in bed."

"I was starting to think of you as a friend, Marianne," Zuleikha jokes.

"Oh, but I am. I'm just saying!" Marianne laughs. "Tell you what. I can't tell your hubby what to say to your piano playing, but I think you're just the person I've been looking for to go to movies with. Ron hates chick flicks and Rachel...well, she's out of the house now and thinks she's too old to do anything with Mom, so if you're up for it sometimes, I have Mondays off."

Her first winter in Texas is mild and dry. Apart from a short trip to Washington, D.C. to visit Iskander's parents during the holidays, it passes slowly and methodically, in the kitchen, at the library, in front of the piano.

She makes a new year's resolution to finally master Balakirev's *Islamey*, but as the weeks progress, she finds herself spending more time doubting the foolhardiness of undertaking that enterprise than on her piano bench. She can get through the first section effortlessly, but then has to slow down the tempo to negotiate all the octaves and double notes. It irks her to contemplate that unlike the soldiers whose triumphs in hard-fought battles inspired the composition of such a challenging masterpiece, she might lack the endurance to truly capture its essence by pounding on strings with a hammer. At other times, she feels somewhat grateful that at least she can recognize the limits of her own abilities. She decides she is glad that she isn't like Frances Ha, a character portrayal she and Marianne both immensely enjoyed on screen, but one whose blindness to her own limitations, whose persistence and struggles, are truly foreign to her sensibilities.

One afternoon the following spring, the sky turns menacing into abstract shades of dark gray. As Zuleikha drives home from the library, a woman's voice on her car radio (which by now has discarded all pretense of cooperating and stays permanently on) makes an urgent announcement about a tornado watch. Zuleikha hurries inside their house just as the winds begin to act drunk and disorderly, and then all of nature gets violently ill. She calls Iskander at work, leaves a voice message, tries him again before hanging up. After a while he returns her call, chuckling, saying she had better get used to those "tornado things," because they're just a fact of life in north Texas. And by the way, the shelter is the hallway closet in the middle of the house and away from all the windows, just in case the siren sounds. She can just see the sly smile on his face as he speaks on the phone, the pressed lips.

When the siren does sound, she hides in the closet, feeling alternately ridiculous and terrified while hail rattles the roof. It's the first time she has been inside an enclosed space this small. A black leather jacket hangs in a clear garment bag. She looks closer and sees the thick wide scrapes on the leather. On the shelf are a toolbox and an old compact-disc player. A closer inspection in the space between them reveals a tattered, torn glove. Zuleikha reaches for the glove and picks it up just as lightning strikes nearby and the power goes out. She screams.

After the eye of the storm has passed and electricity has been restored, she sits at the piano, still unsettled, playing short pieces from memory, jumping from one fragment to another, alternately upset with her husband for the chuckle and with his wife for panicking so easily; scolding, willing herself to continue playing.

She lingers on the first of Erik Satie's *Gnossiennes*, a staple at school and a favorite ever since she borrowed a bootleg copy of *The Painted Veil* from Papajaan's store and watched it with her friends from the academy. The piece is dark and simple, nothing like *Islamey*, or even Chopin's *Nocturnes* or Liszt's *Concertos* that still frustrate her to no end, and when she is finished, a voice startles her.

"Amazing," Iskander says. Instead of leaving his car parked outside and coming in through the front door as usual, he has entered through the garage and has been standing in the hallway, listening, for how long she doesn't know. It embarrasses her.

But isn't this the type of affirmation from a man she's dreamed about all these years?

Now her husband comes up and stands behind, his clothes, smelling of the damp air and the rain, brushing against her. He places his hands on her shoulders and says, "That was *stunning*, Zu. And in this weather! I thought I'd walked into a haunted house up on a hill instead of my own."

In an instant the chuckle from earlier is forgiven. His words spark a desire in her, they rekindle the memory of an unforgettable high school chemistry experiment she once observed. A pile of the dangerous but innocuous white powder of that mercury compound (*thio-* something: was it called?) was ignited, and burned with a blue flame at the tip to emerge in the shapeshifting form of a large, winding, pyrotechnical snake, while the students gasped in awe. It even had a fantastical name to boot: the Pharaoh's Serpent. All evening, Zuleikha smolders, she slithers, and she debates. It's about taking the initiative, which until now she hasn't, even though they have been amorous often enough in the way newlyweds are, or are supposed to be. But he's been the one leading, always. It's about her putting an exclamation point at the end of a remarkable evening he started with a simple word that says so much. She wants to show how he has touched her with his appreciation for her one true gift, which is indubitably not her culinary prowess. It's about the way these poignant moments always resolve themselves in her favorite movies.

When the pregnancy is confirmed a few weeks later, she confides in Marianne with all the confidence in the world that the baby had to have been conceived that night, and on no other.

Maybe that's what it is, that she can never be sure of her own position in this post-racial, post-colonial, post-modern, post-everything world in which she gives birth to her son. When it's all said and done, Zuleikha asks herself, isn't life all about trying to make things a little better for your children than your parents could for you? And how many of us even get to do that? Papajaan lost one of his two stores while transitioning from the cassette/video tape era to the CD/DVD one. Yet, he somehow managed to not only get that Casio, but also send his two children to bilingual schools, pay bribes to get Jameel an interview with the civil service after he completed his diploma in Farsi despite complaining about it, bitterly, all the time, and also manage to somehow save for her wedding. Papajaan did that by risking jail, black-marketing books, movies and albums deemed immoral, and therefore banned, by the omnipotent Telecommunications Authority. He used to wink—*don't let your mother find out*—whenever Zuleikha slipped one of those books or DVDs into her study bag.

In the end, however, this little arrangement between doting father and loving daughter was not something that could be managed surreptitiously and without generating scandal and enmity. The parents of one of Zuleikha's classmates, Parveen, discovered that their daughter had watched a contraband western film with Zuleikha, one about adultery no less. Instead of wearing the usual *dupatta* just over her hair, Parveen had to hide behind a *niqaab* for two weeks in the sear of summer, one that covered her entire head and face and the eggplant-colored bruises all over it. Papajaan had his license revoked and his business shut down, although he miraculously avoided jail, thanks to Jameel's civil-service connections. On the day his remaining store sold, he came home and announced, "It was all going to go away to the hocus pocus internet thing anyway, but at least Allah let me save up for the wedding. Now I can go back to doing what I always liked," (he meant carpentry, of course!), and went in search of his tools.

"That's a fascinating story," Marianne says, in between sips of coffee, while Zuleikha cradles her mug of tea. They're lounging around one muggy Monday afternoon in the drawing room of Marianne's chaotic Las Colinas condominium. Dresses, underwear and lingerie hang from the backs of chairs and the arms of the sofa on which they sit. Scattered on the floor lie knickknacks, magazines, items of makeup, and an unconnected printer. In a haphazardly cleared spot in the middle, Wasim reclines in his foldable rocking seat, occasionally reaching up to grab his toy rainforest friends, and the two women take turns swaying him.

"But whenever you talk about leaving things better for your kids, you have to define what's better, don't you? That's the rub, isn't it?"

"I'm not sure what you mean." Zuleikha detects an ambiguity just beyond the surface of her friend's words.

"Oh, rub? I'm not talking about barbeque, or even massages! But take Ron, for example. He has started pestering me to move to Omaha with him. Omaha, for God's sake! But that's where he thinks he'll get transferred to, and he'd like me to move there with him because he wants to get married. So the decision for me, at some point, becomes: do you continue to go to bed with your own dissatisfactions, or trade them for someone else's? What's better for me and my daughter: me staying here, near her, while she's still in college, or—"

Zuleikha, despite knowing Ron only in passing and no more than Marianne knows Iskander, nevertheless breaks into an excited little clap. "Oh my God, that's great, Marianne! I mean, I'll miss you, for sure, but really, that sounds so exciting."

"Exciting—really? With my track record? You gotta be kidding! When there's only two more years left of helping your child, you start feeling proud of yourself, and then you think, now I have to give up having things my way." Marianne rolls her eyes and makes a sweeping gesture across the room, "And for what? Your little monster needs a diaper change, by the way."

Zuleikha puts her son on the sofa next to her before reaching for her diaper bag, while Wasim wiggles and warbles. "But Marianne!" she says. "That sounds like you're ready to renounce the ideas of marriage, love, all the things—"

"I've done love, I've done marriage. I did those things when doing them was fun. I've also done parenting. But you know what I haven't done a lot of? Marianne, that's what! And that might sound a little strange to you now, but believe me, when you get to be my age, you'll understand."

Zuleikha lets Marianne's words sink into her as she places Wasim back on his chair and hands him a bottle, then navigates her way through the clutter to discard the dirty diaper in Marianne's trash bin.

"Okay, that's enough about me," says Marianne, "What does *better* mean to you?"

"I don't know. I just want Wasim to grow up happy, I guess. But to Iskander, it means opening something called a 529 account. He says it's important to start saving right away, so that not just college, but also graduate school is taken care of."

"So what's the problem?"

"What worries me is Iskander planning out Wasim's

childhood in its entirety: Montessori at three, he says. Tennis and golf lessons before elementary school, he says, to see if we have a prodigy on our hands. And do you want to know why those two sports? Because they are 'individual events where you don't have to get along with teammates and therefore no one can bring you down, and also because you can make a good bit of money if you turn out any good.'"

Marianne breaks out into shrieks of laughter. She bends over Wasim and starts cooing to the child: "You're in trouble, little fella! Aren't you? Aren't you? Yes you are!"

Wasim wildly flails his arms and legs and reaches for Marianne's fingers dangling over his face.

"And Iskander's mother," Zuleikha continues morosely, "who's flying in from D.C. every two or three weeks now to see her grandson—not that I mind, because she really helps with Wasim—I never thought I'd say this, but it does start to wear on you after a while when your mother-in-law reminds you every chance she gets how lucky you are to have a husband so prudent, so wise, such a great family man, etc., etc."

"I never thought you'd have anything but nice things to say about your mother-in-law either. Just goes to show how far you've come since I first met you, and I think I deserve at least some credit for that."

"Cut it out, will you?" Zuleikha says, and it occurs to her that she does, indeed, sound more like Marianne lately.

"Well, when will you talk to Iskander about what *you* want?"

And so, a few weeks later, on the drive back home in Iskander's Lexus after dropping off his parents at the airport, Zuleikha does bring up the subject.

"Not to be pushy or anything," she says, "but whenever I hear you and your parents discuss all the things you want Wasim to do, I want to ask: does it matter what I think?"

"Of course it does! What do you have in mind?"

"Well, the boy was born in the land of the free, so let him run free when he's young."

"Zu, Zu, let me stop you right there. Remember what I said about my work, how it can all be explained in zeroes and ones? Can you explain what you mean, exactly, in simple, concrete sentences?"

Zuleikha hears the impatience and condescension in his tone and feels extremely uncomfortable. She fastens her stare on the radio antenna outside that vibrates monotonously as they roll along Highway 114, and exhorts her inner Marianne to find its voice.

"Is this about cricket?" Iskander asks. She notes a cunning little smile appear out of nowhere and spread between his clear black eyes, as if he's an attorney who has just cracked a witness under oath, and what he says next makes Zuleikha feel as if he has decided to grill that witness—her, his own wife—with a prosecutorial zeal.

"You want him to play cricket, don't you? Piano and cricket—Allahu Akbar!"

"But that's not it!" Zuleikha protests. "Growing up, we used to see these American shows on TV; eight, nine-year olds, surfing. Kids! No older than us, and they looked so happy."

"See, that's what you get from watching crap on TV, all those feel-good propaganda programs meant to show how good life is—was—in this country. That world's gone.

We're all interconnected now, Zu—you know that!—and that boy's gotta learn how to compete in the modern world. Besides," Iskander smiles and shakes his head, "have you looked around? Where's he gonna go surfing in Texas?"

"I understand what you're saying, and I know you mean well," she replies, carefully measuring her words. "It's just that I think...I mean, if you impose so many rules on him at so early an age, how can he grow up to be anything other than a robot? Is that what you...what we want from our child?"

Iskander takes his hands off the wheel and raises them all the way up to his ears in a display of exasperation, before flinging them back down. His action causes the car to swerve violently to the left. Zuleikha lets out a horrified gasp and instinctively throws her left hand into the space between the driver's and passenger seats. The terrifying noise of tires screeching rings out, followed by that of horns blaring. Iskander mutters "Shit" under his breath and brings the car back onto its original lane. In the backseat, Wasim is awakened from his nap and begins crying.

Iskander, visibly shaken, slows his car down and turns the blinker on, signaling his intent to cross over from the middle to the right lane. A sport utility vehicle pulls up to their left and then slows down abruptly, keeping pace with their vehicle, and the sound of its horn is heard again. Zuleikha sees the passenger side window of the SUV rolled down, and the driver—a man in a hat and sunglasses—raising his hand in an obscene gesture.

"Yeah, yeah...you too, asshole," Iskander hisses, returning the gesture. He looks extremely angered, in a way Zuleikha has never observed before; now, as the other vehicle begins to pull away, Iskander presses his own horn, sending Wasim into a new fit of pique.

"Stop the car," she says. "I have to check on Wasim. Please! Stop the car."

Iskander takes the next exit and finally pulls up at the parking lot of a fast food restaurant off the service road. She gets out of the car and into the back seat.

Running his fingers through his hair, ruining the neat parting along the middle, Iskander bemoans, "Typical Texas hothead!"

She wants to ask Iskander why he isn't one as well. But she doesn't. She hides whatever agitation she feels, and only reproaches him in her heart.

When Marianne announces she will be moving to Nebraska after all, Zuleikha puts on a brave face and proclaims she always knew Marianne would.

"I guess we're all suckers for the love scam, aren't we," Marianne says. "But you have to be, don't you? What else is there?"

Zuleikha can't decide who Marianne's questions are meant for, but her friend is already listing all the tasks she has to accomplish before the move.

A month later—during which Zuleikha visits her friend as often as she can—Marianne is gone.

Weekday mornings, before the sun gets too scalding, she pushes Wasim in his stroller along Campion Trail, but she no longer goes all the way to the Royal Lane underpass, turning around at the Spring Trail Park instead. The bulletin board at the edge of the park is aflutter with flyers for lessons in hula hooping, French cooking, and Mandarin speaking, and after Zuleikha masters the skill of creating tear-off strips with a phone number at the bottom, she pins her own flyer for piano lessons among the rest.

Her first student is a nine-year-old boy, thin and lily-white, with much too earnest a personality for a child his age. He is dropped off at her house for his forty-five minute lesson every Saturday morning, when Iskander takes Wasim to the local driving range. Then she acquires a few other students, and eventually a man who runs a company called Home Music Teachers calls out of the blue. His name is Heath and he says he's been hearing good things about her. He schedules an interview and afterwards proposes that she join his team of instructors, promising a steadier stream of business, regular recital opportunities for her students, and a higher rate than she's been able to earn by teaching solo.

"What do you think?" she asks Iskander over lunch the next weekend.

"That's an interesting idea," her husband replies. After a brief pause, he nods in agreement and says, "Actually, I think that's a very good idea. You'll get to do more of what you love, and I'll have more time to hit the range with Wasim. He's getting the hang of it. Aren't you, Wasim? You love to try to whack golf balls, right?"

At the mention of golf balls, Wasim excitedly leaps off his chair and makes a mad dash for the hallway closet.

"He's not even three. How can he get the hang of a golf swing already?" Zuleikha asks.

"Do you know how old Tiger was when he started?" Iskander asks. "Trust me, he can. Look at him go."

Wasim stands just outside the breakfast nook, taking

exaggerated swings with his club. Zuleikha gives him a meaningful stare and motions him back to the table.

"Not now, Wasim," Iskander tells their son, before turning to her. "But anyway, that's beside the point. The point is that we can put off having another baby for a bit; I'm having too much fun with this one right now. And maybe this will cure whatever's been bothering you since your friend left."

"I don't know," she demurs. "I'm torn. I mean, I'm excited, of course, but sometimes this sounds a bit daunting."

"Well, you don't *have* to do it. But if you need help with something, like opening a small business account, or how to itemize everything, I'm your man," Iskander smiles.

He does not let her embark on her new venture before ferreting out the legitimacy of Heath's enterprise, however, or making a personal visit to the daycare that Zuleikha has selected for Wasim, claiming that such actions merely constitute the duties of a diligent husband and father.

Within a few months, Zuleikha ends up with a roster of no fewer than a dozen budding musicians, some of whom come to her home, some she visits at theirs.

Around Labor Day, one of the children at the daycare turns three, and Wasim receives an invitation to the birthday party. It's on a Saturday afternoon, but Iskander, saddled with weekend coverage, has to go the office. Zuleikha walks the half-mile with her son to an unfamiliar part of the subdivision. The two-story house stands on a double lot, looming large like a temple to an unknown god, incongruous to the rest of the neighborhood full of single-story, sprawling ranch-style brick homes. It has an asymmetrical façade, floor-to-ceiling windows, strong, geometric lines, bright whitewashed walls and tinted windows, a front yard full of orchids and rockrose.

By the time they arrive, there are already several cars parked in front and on the driveway, and Zuleikha has to ring the bell a second time, before the door is opened by a rangy man with closely cropped red-orange hair sprinkled with white, and a craggy face. The man bends down and says to Wasim with a pretend scowl and comic hostility, "Who might you be?"

Wasim, quite shaken, takes a step back, leans in close to his mother and slips his hand in between her legs and around her jeans.

The man stands up and holds the door open for them. "Aw, don't be scared. Come in! I'll show you where Jamieson is." He extends his hand to Zuleikha. "I apologize. Patrick."

Zuleikha is immediately struck by a sense of knowing Patrick—his sharp jawline and nose, his intense eyes, and the weathered lines of a face that appears to receive more than its fair share of time in the sun—from somewhere. He brings to her mind the vague memory of the cunning, highly intelligent villain from some long forgotten movie, whose defeat cannot be brought about by mere intelligence, resolve, and heroic acts, but only with guile and deceit that in turn defiles the hero and leaves him bereft of his own worthy ideals. She introduces herself and Wasim and they follow Patrick inside. They walk past the dining room, the kitchen, and the den where Jamieson's older sister—whom Zuleikha recognizes from the daycare and whose name she thinks is Cassandra but can't recall

33

for sure—plays with her friends. Lances of light penetrate through the numerous skylights shaped like squares and rectangles and circles and ovals. The light refracts off the polished floors and off walls concave and convex. They enter a large, L-shaped room in the back. A knot of people stands by a glass sliding door, watching the children play outside.

The doorbell rings and Patrick excuses himself, but Zuleikha spots Juliet—Jamieson's mother—in the room. Names and greetings are hastily exchanged, the door is slid open to let Wasim out, closed again, and from behind the glass Zuleikha watches her son disappear in the jungle of colorful shorts and t-shirts as inside, the fragments of conversation among the adults, which halted momentarily with their arrival, pick up again. A group of four spiritedly discusses a reality show. Two other men and three other women—including Juliet—talk about a TV special on Afghanistan. Zuleikha, on account of knowing only Juliet, drifts closer to this second group. A woman in this group vents about how frustrating it is to see her tax dollars being wasted on such a hopeless situation, so far away from home, when local teachers are making do without essential supplies and textbooks.

"Tell me about it," one of the men responds in a griping tone, and the first woman starts speaking again, then stops. A quick glance passes between her and Juliet, and then an almost imperceptible shift in the conversation seems to take place. The woman rolls her eyes and says, "All I'm saying is that I'm tired of all this fighting. Aren't ya'll?"

"I think the whole world is tired of all this fighting," Juliet says with a charming gaiety. "And while that is a fascinating topic and all, it's a birthday party, people. Excuse me; I have to go order the pizza. Will one of you help me take some water out to the kids? They must all be so thirsty out there."

Zuleikha says she'd love to, and Juliet thanks her, adding, "And while we're doing that, you must share the secrets of your skin. Goodness, just look at it!"

After the kids have all taken their bottles of water, Juliet goes back inside, while Zuleikha, left behind leaning against the droning air conditioner, strains her neck to make sure she is out of sight of the people inside the sliding glass door. She lingers in the backyard and watches the children play. In Pakistan, she would barely glance at the front-page headlines while retrieving the newspaper, but before handing it to Papajaan, she would dig out the Arts and Culture section to check on the new movie releases and museum exhibits. She does the same with the Sunday paper in Dallas. Consequently, she has never possessed insight into the political hot-button issues, and now she realizes that she has little to say to the strangers she met inside. She decides she doesn't care if she talks to anybody else or not. She'll wait for the pizza, the song and the cake, and then take Wasim home.

She remembers an incident with Iskander earlier that summer. They were sitting in their dining room on a Sunday morning, having breakfast. The paper was strewn all over the table. Wasim had oatmeal bits in his hair, and worse, he paid no mind to her when she pointed that out to him.

"You really need a haircut," Zuleikha told him. But then a story in Art and Life caught her eyes. It announced the winner of the recently completed Van Cliburn piano competition in Fort Worth.

"Twenty-one! Can you imagine, winning at twenty-one?" she asked Iskander, pointing to the story.

Looking up from the front page, Iskander glanced at the section she held in her hands. "Why didn't you tell me? We could have gone to see it. I'm sure it can't be too hard to get tickets to a piano competition."

"I didn't know, but next time I will. And it's not just any piano competition, but one of most prestigious ones! Sir Pendleton used to tell us we should all aspire to be in an event like that someday, and nothing less. Not that any of us ever did. But he would be so excited if I ever told him I went to see the Van Cliburn competition," she gushed. "I've told you about Sir Pendleton, haven't I? The one who had all those stories, who used to say all those funny things, like" —she tried to mimic an English accent—"'find yourself by losing yourself,' or, 'if you stop clutching your heart with your hands every time something goes wrong and let your heart hold your hands instead, the piano will play itself.'"

"Uh-huh," Iskander replied, "he sounds like a teacher all right."

"He's the one who told us about the legend of Van Cliburn, about how he won the competition from Khrushchev during the Cold War; it's such a great story!"

"Didn't Khrushchev have better things to do during the Cold War than go to a piano competition? One of his lackeys—yes, I can believe that, but Khrushchev? Come on."

"But he did, I'm telling you. He just decided that Van Cliburn was the best...you know what, let me back up..."

"Let me back up and tell you a really interesting story

about Khrushchev and Kennedy," Iskander smiled and said.

A tiny amp of anger surged across her brain then. She wanted to tell Iskander off, but the right words sounded all wrong in her head. She got up and grabbed Wasim. "You know what, that's enough! You're getting in the shower, now!"

And with that, she had dragged her son out of the dining room, fuming as much at herself as at her husband.

Now Patrick steps outside through a side door near the far corner of the wall. From where Zuleikha stands, he appears visibly agitated. Unaware of her presence, he vigorously shakes his head for a moment as if to rid his thoughts of the cobweb of ill-will in which they have tangled themselves, and proceeds to take deep breaths and stick his fingers out one by one. By the time he counts to ten, however, his expression undergoes a remarkable alteration before Zuleikha's very eyes. He calls out Jamieson and his face breaks into a smile, which eclipses the lines and the cragginess. His son runs to him and eagerly pulls him by his hand, coaxing him to discard his sandals and join the group of boys. Barefoot, they resume with him their feverish chase of a soccer ball; one giant surrounded by a hooting and howling Lilliputian cluster, playing according to rules alien to the game and perhaps to the players themselves.

Patrick spots Zuleikha and waves at her while playing. She waves back and continues to watch, fascinated by the shift in Patrick's personality. Unlike Iskander, who never seems to relinquish his position of paternal authority when entertaining Wasim, Patrick shouts and makes extravagant gestures as much as the children do and appears to be just as full of silliness.

After a while he stops playing, bends down to say something to Jamieson, and walks over to her.

"I know you told me your name when you came in, but I'm afraid my vanity will be crushed if I try to pronounce it now. Mine's Patrick, by the way."

She tells him her name and observes him rolling it over his tongue, savoring it like chocolate, but he does not say it out loud.

Instead, he says, "I'm sorry; we're usually better hosts than this. Did anybody offer you anything to drink?"

"The kids took all the water, but if you can get me some, thank you."

"Juliet has a strict policy of not serving our adult guests anything besides adult beverages, and I am not in the mood to have to explain anything else to her today." He tries—she thinks—to sound as if he and Juliet have been married long enough to manufacture innocent insults about each other, but the sourness suddenly reappears on his face. "So, your choices are beer, our special Long Island iced tea—it's blue, that's what so special about it—or something even stronger. Or you can choose to die of thirst." As an afterthought, he adds, "Unless it's a religious thing? In which case I'm sure she will be happy to make an exception."

Zuleikha laughs and says no, it isn't, and yes, maybe she'll try the iced tea, and when he leaves to get the drinks, she leans her head back, inhaling the warm air, thinking how much she prefers it over the mechanical chill of the inside, even if it causes beads of perspiration to form on her forehead. A minute or two later, she senses Patrick's presence beside her, and it gives her a strange catch at the heart. She opens her eyes to find him holding two plastic cups of punch.

"You weren't joking about the blue."

He makes a show of offering her a cup and taking it back, before handing it over.

"Now these should be illegal, and I'm certain the government's spying on our household to find the secret recipe. So by consuming this, you risk becoming an accomplice. Don't say I didn't warn you."

She feels a little bewildered and doesn't know what to say.

"That was a joke! You know, the NSA?"

"I have no idea what you're talking about."

"Let's drink to that, shall we?" Patrick says with a broad smile, and they raise their cups.

The boys surround them suddenly, pleading with Patrick to join their play again. Zuleikha finds it amusing that even Wasim, who suffered through his initial encounter with Patrick with suspicion and anxiety, now tugs at him like the rest.

Patrick plays for a few more minutes while Zuleikha continues to watch, sipping her cocktail. Then he feigns exhaustion and excuses himself from the boys despite their protestations, making his way back to her.

"They'll sleep well tonight, eh?" he says.

"I sure hope so."

"Your name," he says suddenly, "surely it means something, or has some story behind it? I mean, don't beautiful, exotic names like that stand for a warrior's will or a saint's humility or some other noble virtue that a parent or a grandparent values above all else?"

"Very good, Patrick," Zuleikha says. His name, on the

other hand, feels sturdy escaping her lips, like the furniture Papajaan made for their home, all from teak. "There're several stories, actually, behind my name, and in them, the principal character is not a heroine, but a villain—villainess? They're about a different kind of tension between Muslims and Jews than what seems to have become more common now. You wouldn't care; you're neither Muslim nor Jewish, are you? You have a very beautiful house, by the way."

"No, I'm neither, and well, I could do the proper thing and tell you it's only my third noblest creation—after the kids, of course—but who am I kidding? I was the one who drew this house up on paper, had the old one demolished and stood here and oversaw construction every single day for the better part of a year, helped the electricians and laid the tiles with my own two hands, whereas making the kids took...how long? How long does it take a man to do his part in the making of a couple of babies anyway?" He flashes a wicked little smile that reduces his age by a good many years. "On second thought, don't answer that. Or tell anyone else how I really feel. And don't think that I didn't see what you did there. You know, change the topic."

"Oh, I didn't mean to. It's just that those silly stories are too embarrassing to tell someone you've just met."

"Well, I can't pretend that stories are my métier, but now I'm *really* curious."

Zuleikha steals a glance at Patrick, catches him staring straight back into her eyes with mischief, and is unable to divert the conversation yet again.

"Okay, fine. They are about the wife of a rich Egyptian—we call him Azeez, the Jews call him Potiphar. A couple without children."

"And this wife is Zuleikha?"

"Of course, it's about her, remember! And here comes Joseph, Jacob's son, whose brothers hate him because he is the favorite, right? So they throw him into a well. That's in every Abrahamic book of God, isn't it? Anyway, Joseph is rescued, sold into slavery, and he ends up at the house of Azeez, where Zuleikha falls in love with him. There are several stories from this point. She tries to, um, seduce him. But he's Joseph, right? He doesn't allow that. One day she tears off his tunic and they're both caught. It becomes a case of he says, she says, and in the end her husband Azeez has to forgive her, all that. Now, there's another story about how she ends up adopting a girl, because Joseph won't, you know, give her a child, and in an ironic twist her adopted daughter is the one that ends up marrying Joseph and having his children. But *my* favorite is the one where Zuleikha's friends mock her for falling so in love with a Jewish slave."

"Wait! So your favorite is the story without the stripping and the sex?"

Zuleikha makes a face of affectionate admonishment, thinks—even as she is making that face—that the gesture is one only a girl much younger than her could be forgiven for making.

"As I was saying: these friends that tease and mock her...she invites them to her house. She gives each an apple and a knife, tells them she needs help. And while they're paring the fruit, she has Joseph called into the room."

"Bravo!" says Patrick with a mock clap. "And the fine Egyptian ladies all cut their hands when they see the handsome Jewish slave..."

"Hey, it's my story! But yes, they bleed and understand how hard it is for their friend Zuleikha to live with what she cannot have, even though she seemingly has it all. They never make fun of her again. The end."

Patrick scratches the stubble on his chin and settles into a broody countenance.

"Those are the best kinds of stories, aren't they? Beautiful, age-old conundrums...to remind us there's no new difficulty, happiness, or emotion to be experienced; that someone's already felt every which way before."

"That's a rather dreary way of looking at things, isn't it?"

"Yes, I suppose it is," he says. "So what does *our* Zuleikha do? Seduce the handyman, the postman, the pool guy?"

Caught unawares, Zuleikha tries to take on an air of quiet dignity, as if his insinuation is an affront to her integrity. It occurs to her that she has never been this flirtatious, that only some combination of sun and drink could have caused it. But she has absorbed far too much of the former and one too many of the latter to now recapture her dignity. The boys continue to play, oblivious to the two grown-ups, their little shrieks of joy and complaint pinpricks to her being.

"She does no such thing!" says Zuleikha. "She and her husband have a son. He's the reason she's here. She takes care of him and gives piano lessons on the side, and she has a hard enough time juggling the two."

He gives her a long, curious glance as if seeing her anew. She is profoundly aware of his gaze, and it makes her blush.

"No kidding. The piano, of all things! Do you teach the

five-finger technique, starting with C-D-E, or do it the old-fashioned way from A to G?"

Laughing out loud, she says, "You know, nobody else has asked me that! Do you play?"

"They should, but then again, I was never any good, so what do I know? To answer your question: not really, I gave up. I wish the kids played, though, but they're into other things."

The sliding glass door to the backyard slides open again. Through it, Juliet's voice rings out. It is time to cut the cake, sing.

It takes another announcement before the children stop to gather by the door. Patrick seems oddly occupied. Finally, he says with some hesitation, "I've always wanted to pick up the piano again. In fact, maybe I will, do something for myself for a change." He flashes that wicked smile again, and adds, "Which means I might be in the market for a piano teacher, but only if she teaches the basics the proper way..."

"I do start at the A, but are you serious? I mean, I've only taught kids and a couple of old ladies trying to recapture old glory."

"Well, I can't act like an old lady, but I can still act like a kid sometimes. Does that count? Or are you just patently opposed to the idea?"

"Of course not. I'm busy, but I can take on another student, I think. Especially if I don't have to remind you to practice."

"You won't, I promise. And I'm glad to hear it. May I call you for an appointment when I'm in the office and in front of my calendar?"

***

She returns home with Wasim to find Iskander home from work on the couch, watching television, the remains of the previous night's dinner on the coffee table and picked through. The sight suddenly exasperates her.

"Do you know the meaning of my name?" she asks him later as they get ready for bed.

"What?"

"I said: do you know where my name comes from? Like your name comes from Alexander, right? Do you know where mine comes from?"

"What kind of question is that?" Iskander says. "It's a perfectly fine name. Did someone at the party make fun of it or something?"

"No. I'm just curious if you've ever been curious, that's all."

"No. Should I have? Where *does* your name come from?"

"Never mind, don't know what I was thinking. I must be tired."

After Iskander has fallen asleep, Zuleikha continues to replay her conversation with Patrick in her mind, dissecting every glance, every nuance, not a little surprised at the impression left upon her by a person she had initially mistaken for possessing a decidedly prickly demeanor. It occurs to her that she never saw Patrick speaking with Juliet at the party. Even when they were singing *Happy Birthday* to their son, the two stood pointedly apart and did not look in each other's direction. Away from their home now, Zuleikha has no problem believing that the party was just a big show for the benefit of their children and the guests, and she falls asleep to the murmur of a restless question: how long the two have been drifting.

Patrick calls her Monday morning to make the appointment. Zuleikha has spent the better part of the prior day and a half imagining just such a call, but actually receiving it and hearing Patrick's voice again make her heart leap.

At the piano, he is a basket of contradictions. During the first lesson, he seems to possess a rudimentary grasp of theory, but then surprises her with a touching rendition of the third movement of Chopin's second Sonata.

"Are you sure you're not just pretending to need lessons?" Zuleikha asks him.

"I wouldn't dream of it," Patrick replies. "See the thing about me is that I liked that piece so much that I decided I'd learn to play it. So, I memorized the notes and kept at it, listening and practicing, listening and practicing, until I got it down. But what comes before or after it? That I can't even think of trying, because I can't sight read worth a lick."

After observing other signs of rust—uncoordinated technique, poor timing, and indeed, poor sight-reading ability—she decides he is telling the truth. But when she reaches across the piano for a demonstration, his intake of breath does not escape her attention.

Over the next month, although Patrick has to reschedule his lessons a couple of times, he does actually manage to make time for his one session every week. She juggles her calendar for his sake without irritation, keeping open, as much as possible, the half hours following his lessons, offering him tea with the excuse of having to make some for herself anyway. The sight of him, taking to the keys with gusto and pouring over the sight refresher material with care, fills her with pleasure. He accepts his shortcomings with cheerful resignation, reminding her of the gallant pageantry he displayed playing with children.

But if that lightheartedness fills her with good humor, it is the conversations with him that continue to linger within the waves and eddies of her thoughts long after he has departed.

Her lesson is his weekly dose of medicine, Patrick tells her. And that he's glad she doesn't have a clue what the NSA stands for.

The shape of those conversations does not assume the trajectory of a straight line, but rather the meandering path of two people revealing the ennui of each other's lives with gradual, apprehensive unmasking. By sharing anecdotes from work (he is part-owner of a private construction firm,) Patrick offers Zuleikha glimpses into a quick, curious mind with dark corners. She finds herself wanting to explore and fill them with her own light, brushing aside the vexing thought that she's seeking to annex a portion of his life—a portion not unlike a remote and yet strategic island belonging to a powerful nation—to her own, attention-hungry one.

His invitation to lunch follows naturally.

They meet late, after one-thirty, at a Greek Café off Macarthur, on the south side of Highway 114 instead of north, which is always busier. The place is empty but for a pair of suits, stacks of paper spread out in front of them, engrossed in conversation. Patrick requests that the waiter show them to a booth, sits beside her instead of across from her, and as soon as the waiter leaves, leans and tries to kiss her.

She puts her hand on his shoulder and pushes him back, while pulling herself back at the same time. "Patrick!"

At that moment, the waiter returns with water.

"Give us a few minutes, please," Patrick says to the man, before turning to her. "Have I been misreading you that poorly, then? You mean to tell me that you're happy with what you have?"

"I don't know if I can call myself completely happy, I don't know if anybody can. Happiness is such a fleeting, opaque concept, don't you think? But I also know that I shouldn't complain about what I do have. I have no right to complain."

"And yet here you are."

She does not know what to say. Patrick, too, becomes silent, and a cloud hangs over his face. This overwhelms her and she wants to touch his face. But he soon composes himself, talks to her about the menu, signals for the waiter.

After the orders are placed, he reaches into his pocket and pulls out a yellow and black pouch.

"No, please!" Zuleikha protests.

"This didn't cost anything—I mean I didn't buy this; it's just something I've wanted to give you for some time now. Before you say no, will you at least see what's inside?"

She pries apart the mouth of the pouch and pulls out seashells. She lays them, one by one, on the table between their place settings.

"We drove to Kaladesi from Disneyworld last year," Patrick says, "and during that trip Juliet and I both realized we'd stopped loving each other. I take that back—that we hated each other. But she'll never agree to a divorce. It's complicated between us."

"I'm sorry."

"No need. After fighting with her all night at the hotel, I took the kids out to the beach and we spent the morning collecting shells. I bought three pouches from a street vendor, we put the shells in, and each made a wish. That was Cassie's idea and Jamieson liked it too, so we all did it. God, I don't even know what happened to theirs—probably lost in the crates of toys. But mine...I was alone, confused, stressed out and horny and angry, had been all of those things for some time and knew then that I was going to be that way for a lot longer." He laughs. "And I saved this to someday give to the next special woman I met."

Zuleikha lets him kiss her then. The strange aftertaste of coffee passes from his mouth into hers, but it does not offend her as much as when she'd tried coffee herself.

Two weeks pass. They continue the lessons, they talk, but they also kiss, and she lets Patrick embrace her, hold her, and grope her, even though she does not make what a romance novel might call the final submission to his passion. Nor to her own, which, with each passing day, she begins to suspect, is as great as his, if not greater. But her life is not a sentimental story, or a movie adapted from a sentimental story, and she is acutely aware of the expectations of her station in life: her fidelity not just to Iskander but also to her parents and her responsibilities to Wasim. And, too, the traditions of her culture, not to mention a deep-seated, subliminal fear of Allah's wrath, hold her back.

But in the end, they only manage to hold her back for two weeks.

When she does yield, it doesn't happen the way Patrick has suggested: by the two of them checking into a hotel room one afternoon after she has tucked Wasim away at the daycare. It does not even happen the way she has already come close to letting happen, more than once, in their guest bedroom, as if committing that physical act there, somehow, would save some semblance of sanctity in her marriage—something that she has come to decide is a purely metaphysical concept. No, it happens the way it happens, in the throes of a delirious mayhem, when after lunch one day, as Wasim is down for his nap at the other corner of the house, she finds herself leading Patrick into the master bedroom. Once they are there, the crux of a crisis feels resolved; the man is the man and the woman is the woman, and there is only one thing left for them to do, and only one question remaining: how that thing is to be done. He goes about it in ways that make her feel as if no less than a gold medal is at stake. He wins her like a prize.

Afterward, she is amused by the cylindrical imprints—glaringly whiter than the rest of his body—of swimming trunks on Patrick's naked buttocks on her bed, and that bed no longer appears to be the same one she has slept on for years. The odd sight of scattered clothes on the floor, hers and his, suddenly reminds her of Marianne's condominium. That, and the wanton image of the woman in the dresser mirror, makes her suddenly pine for Marianne's throaty laugh. Should she resume email correspondence with her? But then she decides it is just as well that they lost touch, because she could not admit the act she just committed to anyone, not even Marianne.

And that's how she and Patrick go about it. Haphazardly. With no rhyme and no reason, without the faintest regard for the season. Patrick isn't virtuous like Joseph, so she, Zuleikha, doesn't have to be desperate like Zuleikha. He comes to her house. They play her Story & Clark to pieces. They make love. Once, in the middle of their lovemaking, the tune to *Grandpa's Clock* rings out on the piano in the living room, rendering them both stunned and silent. Zuleikha hurriedly dresses herself, motions Patrick to do the same and wait. She gently extricates herself from her bedroom, compliments Wasim for taking to the piano on his own and for the playing itself, and lures her son to the kitchen with the promise of a treat while Patrick surreptitiously makes his escape.

Next week, Patrick rents a room in a Las Colinas hotel. She feels conspicuous as they check in, while he points to the enclosed elevator lobby and comments that despite being excellent in terms of fire safety, it's an eyesore. Glass! Didn't anyone tell them about glass—he exclaims in horror—so that people can look out while they're rising up to their floors? Once inside the room, he claims that its aesthetics are offensive and would normally suffocate him, and that he can only breathe the air in it because it now carries the scent of her body. She laughs and puts her finger on his lips and taps his wristwatch. Their lovemaking is a juxtaposition of contortions and configurations, but in the end it is a confirmation—of the raw vitality of reckless living, and its utter shamelessness. She marvels at the ironies of the shamelessness of making love to a man not her husband.

They continue to—when pressed for time—have trysts at her home. Now that the two are intimate, they no longer speak about their obligations to their immediate families. They either simply share inanities, or talk about movies during lulls in their lovemaking; they have that in common. Once, they skip sex altogether, and meet in uptown Dallas to take in a matinee at the Angelika.

At other times, when Iskander's parents visit and Zuleikha is more mindful of the time, she and her lover meet for lunch—just to be able to see each other—at obscure, tucked-away bistros and cafes that he suggests, places she never knew existed in this corner of the world where she now lives.

More and more, they neglect their lessons. She refuses the gifts he tries to give her and tells him she will never see him again if he insists on them, knowing that she lacks the intestinal fortitude to follow through. She shares with Patrick more about her family in Pakistan than she has ever cared to tell her Pakistani-American husband. Patrick tells her about growing up off the coast of Newfoundland, learning to catch capelin and cod, haddock and swordfish, of forgoing universities closer to home in favor of crossing the pond all the way to Ireland, to attend University College Cork, just so he could get away, build a life different from his brothers' and father's and grandfather's, who had all only been one thing— fishermen. He talks about how he ended up in Irving, Texas. His firm is engaged in building office towers, and here it's mostly been all about granite and glass, that's what brings in the green, he says, jokingly, but lately, more and more new clients are wanting some real green too: gardens on rooftops, trellises here and there, which excites him. That excitement, always, comes to rest in her.

Late afternoons, after seeing him, she fiddles with the

volume button on her car radio until the symphony playing on the Classical 101 station is melodious enough for the drive home. She jumps into the shower and scrubs the effervescent glow off her skin, packs away this newfound sensation of bliss in the deepest closet of her soul, plays piano with Wasim, sings with him, and gets ready to see about dinner before her husband returns from work. If Iskander suggests "Let's make love," she feigns exhaustion and manages—most of the time—to fend him off, while contemplating how strange it is that she has come to like sex in more graphic terms than "lovemaking." When unruly thoughts crowd her head, she brushes them aside. What's adultery anyway, she asks herself. A priest might define it with a different set of rules and logic than a politician, whereas a truly honest person might describe it in some other way altogether. But to be happy, she theorizes, you can be bound by no rule whatsoever. She thinks of that thought as an original pearl of enlightenment, a flawless Tahitian gem to be worn snugly around the neck on a thin, nondescript chain that will not distract from the radiant truth it encapsulates, and banishes the idea—when it presents itself—that the same thought might have been in existence for as long as humans have made up rules.

And she can never figure out who she is cheating. Is it Iskander, the man she has decided she can only be grateful to? Or is it the man who loves her to distraction and makes her feel so happy, but upon whom she has no legitimate claim?

But what about cheating herself? She simply cancels that out.

***

One fall morning, Zuleikha wakes up breathless from a dream of running through glorious riots of yellow mustard blooms filling the vast, familiar Swat valley landscape of her childhood with golden froth. She asks Iskander to toast pre-packaged waffles for breakfast, and can hear him playing with Wasim in the kitchen while she lies in bed pondering the absurdity of the dream. It is barely September; the wind outside bays as it does in North Texas for a week or two during the change of season from summer to fall, making the shingles rattle. Even if it rained here in September, mustard season wouldn't arrive for another three months. The thought of rain hits her with poignancy. She tries to get up for a glass of water, but the sudden movement makes her head spin. She faints.

That evening, Iskander Khan takes his wife and son to dinner at their favorite Pakistani Halal restaurant. Zuleikha likes the food here; it's the closest she can get to her mother's cooking in the Dallas-Fort Worth metroplex. It's also a restaurant where they have to wait in line to order, Pakistani street food style. The owner's wife brings the food, places it on their table which is covered in a green and white plastic tablecloth—the colors of the flag of her homeland. She places her hand gently on Zuleikha's back, gives her a knowing smile.

"The *halwa* is on the house tonight, Beti—our gift to you," she says. "Eat up."

Zuleikha does not understand how this woman can already know what she herself didn't twelve hours earlier. Iskander reaches across the table to squeeze her hand.

"Well, we're a little behind schedule," he says,

beaming, "but it was worth it: giving lessons has made you so much happier. And I want you to know that I was never worried."

She asks Patrick to meet at the same Greek Café where they had lunch that first time; it has become their go-to rendezvous site. But unlike the other times, Zuleikha feels surreally conscious of the trapezoid of sunlight illuminating the café when she opens the door, of the discordant half-note of the bell jangling when that door closes behind her.

Half a dozen men gather around a small television mounted at the far corner of the cafe, watching a soccer game, booing, groaning, cheering, making all kinds of noise that she knows are considered perfectly natural by sports enthusiasts, but which to her—right then—seem grossly irrational.

Patrick, already there, ushers her next to him, tells her he's pressed for time and has already ordered for the both of them—her favorite from the menu and his. He puts his arm around her, tries to. She untangles herself, takes his hand in hers and reaches into her purse with the other, and after carefully looking about, pulls out the pregnancy test—a new one she'd taken that morning just for this occasion—and places it in his.

"Oh no," Patrick whispers. He instinctively reaches and puts his arm around her again, and this time, instead of resisting, she reaches for it, clasps his fist and kisses it, starts sobbing into it. "I thought we always took proper precautions."

Zuleikha rubs her eyes and untangles herself again, pointedly moves a few inches farther away from Patrick.

She is grateful they are not sitting across from each other. She stares into her fork as if it is a scepter laden with divine powers.

"It's not yours."

Patrick puts both elbows on the table, an act he usually frowns upon, and rests his chin upon the ball of his fists. He does not say anything. In that position, his quietness seems to envelop him like an impenetrable cocoon. He stares straight into a nothing. She searches his face for a reaction, anything but nothing. She can't take his silence any longer.

"Say something."

He doesn't. The waiter brings their food and sets it on the table, leaves.

"Patrick, please! Unlike you and Juliet, Iskander and I don't really fight. He has an entirely different view of our life and I am quite certain he doesn't think there is anything wrong with our marriage. So he hasn't exactly, you know, not touched me in the past few months."

"You're right," Patrick says finally. "It is wrong of me to expect you to have done anything different. This makes me sad, very sad, but can you understand that I understand—at least I am trying to—what you've been dealing with?"

He reaches for her hand, smothers it in kisses. She starts crying again, rubs her eyes with her napkin. Her *spanakopita* and his *moussaka* sit untouched on the table.

"Patrick, this is why I loved you. We never said those words to each other, because we knew neither one of us could be free to be together, but I did, love you, and this is why, because of who you are. And I want you to know that the person who was in bed with you is not the same person who was in bed with him."

"I'd rather not have that imagery in my mind. But I can't help—"

The men at the corner erupt into a fit of applause and exultation. They jump up and a chair falls to the floor. The manager, an elderly, short-statured, cordial fellow whom Zuleikha has come to know and exchange pleasantries with over the past few months, hurries to the scene, but instead of becoming upset, he breaks into a toothy grin and exchanges hugs and fist-bumps with the men. He retreats to the petite bar at the other corner of the dining room, extracts a bottle of liquor and short plastic cups, and returns to the fans to the accompaniment of noisy cheers.

"I can't help but notice," Patrick says, "that you are already speaking of us in past tense."

"Can't you understand why? Juliet's given birth twice, so you know what's ahead—"

"None of that will stop me from wanting to see you. Or later, after your baby is born. When two people care about each other, they shouldn't stop just because—"

"No, Patrick. No! I'm a wreck already. This can't continue—it's not good for the baby," she points to her belly. "Or fair to Iskander, for that matter. Remember what I said? That happiness is such a fleeting thing? I said it lightly then, trying to sound more profound than I actually am, not really grasping what those words meant, but I believe it more than ever now. I'm sorry. I can't see you under the pretense of piano lessons either. I'm sorry for being such a bad teacher. I'm sorry for everything."

The soccer fans sing a jubilant song, punctuating the end of each verse with "Opa!"

It takes every last bit of her willpower not to reach for

and touch Patrick's face. But today, that familiar look of sadness on it doesn't last but a fractional pulse. A sense of resignation seems to issue from somewhere deep inside him and hardens his face into rigid, corrugated lines. For the first time it strikes Zuleikha that Patrick is a good decade older than she is. His eyes narrow, his lips purse, his jaws clench. He stands up and makes way for her. She slides across the booth but finds that her legs have lost the spirit of their most basic function.

He helps her stand up, points to the table and says, "I'll take care of all this. Just go."

They are face to face. Faces they had held in each other's hands, traced with each other's lips. Zuleikha wants to say thank you, but that seems awkward and inappropriate. Saying anything seems inappropriate. She touches his cheek a last time, reaches forward and stands on her toes to give him a kiss, but he turns abruptly just at that moment and the kiss lands on his earlobe. She is besieged by a flash of dismay, but only momentarily; she realizes the intent behind the gesture, accepts it. She turns around and walks toward the door, takes off the last few feet in a stumbling run.

Zuleikha unlearns and relearns the roads of the metroplex so as to avoid as much as possible those that she frequented with Patrick. She drives past hotels where she rendezvoused with him and tries not to think of them, as Patrick the construction professional called them, grotesque external tumors bulging out of the skin of the earth, but as fully functional, sincere and legitimate creations of other people. She goes back to filling her mug with tea brewed with teabags like she always had before

Patrick spoiled her with fine loose-leaf varieties at his favorite cafes. In those ways and others, she unspools the most recent reel of her life and sets about—with a sense of determination she had begun to forget she once possessed—focusing on new scenes in her life. Despite morning sickness and its accompanying fatigue, Wasim's ever-expanding vocabulary and energy and his increasing demands on her time and energy and patience, she keeps a full calendar of lessons. She tackles the unfinished scrapbooks of her son's toddler years with a new zeal, determined to complete them before the need for new ones arise.

But despite how many students she introduces to the grand staff and the bass and treble clefs and how much progress she makes with her scrapbooks and how much love and affection she pours into Wasim, she fails to do the one thing that lies at the heart of everything else she does: she fails to shut off her mind.

It would be funny—Zuleikha thinks—if it weren't so sad: this sense of emptiness and the spirit of life being sucked out of her soul, just as her body fills out again and new life grows in her womb. And how strange it is, she marvels when she is not feeling contempt, that she feels contempt not for herself, nor for Patrick, but for the person that hasn't committed the sin of adultery—her husband, the innocent bystander, standing irreproachable like a towering oak whose roots run deep into the soil and whose limbs are solid and thick, but also dull grey and dry. But therein lies the problem, she knows. She can be grateful to Iskander for shelter from storm, admire him for his ability to withstand the mightiest of winds without getting uprooted, but when it comes to love, she can't love him. It takes a certain person to appreciate and love that oak, perhaps—she can freely admit—someone wiser, calmer than she is. But her heart yearns for a fir that can sway this way and that in the wind, and sway her with it. She tries to forget that image of Iskander; the practical realities of her life demand it. She tries to recall moments of tenderness in their marriage prior to Patrick's incursion into it, but apart from a handful of romantic overtures (she has decided they were more accidental than deliberate), none stand out. She recognizes the manner in which Iskander goes about his life, without shirking any responsibility, by being a dutiful father and husband, and can hear her mother's voice in her head even when not on the phone with her: how many husbands of her friends from high school and the music academy would run to the store at a moment's notice to satisfy her craving for pickles? How many of them would dig through the *Consumer Reports* comparing the safety features of different minivans?

Her only friend during her second trimester is an unusually bitter North Texas winter. The cold grows from December to January to February, as does her belly. The cold settles into her bones, and conspiring with the fetus, finally starts slowing her down. She reduces the number of her students, keeping only the ones that are her favorites.

Suddenly the weather turns. The first weekend of March is balmy, the dazzling cerulean sky mottled with thin white wisps of cloud. Iskander climbs up into the attic and brings down Wasim's old crib, dusts it off and sets it up in the corner of their bedroom that is near her side of the bed. The sight of the crib changes her mood; the moroseness that has been keeping her commune through winter is replaced with restless energy and an intangible sense of optimism.

Late afternoon that Sunday, they are having dinner outside on the patio when Iskander asks Wasim, "So are you happy that you'll be having a little brother instead of a sister?"

"Yes!" Wasim replies excitedly. "Boys are more fun."

Zuleikha laughs, as does Iskander, and she says, "But your little brother will follow you everywhere. He will want to play with you all the time. Then you can't ignore him and go play with Zachary and Andrew and Jamieson and—"

His shock of black hair crowding past the forehead and into his eyes, and between bites of rice and chicken, Wasim says, "Jamieson's daddy likes to kiss Mamajaan."

"What? What did you say, Wasim?" Iskander asks.

Wasim, oblivious to the obvious, repeats the sentence.

The eyes of Wasim's parents meet and unmeet, meet again. Iskander's face curls into the familiar, sly smile; it never completely disappears. He asks Zuleikha nothing. She feels as if she has caught a mad fever, as if her face has given away everything that her husband needs to know.

Iskander wipes his face and stands up, picks up his son and playfully nuzzles the boy's chest. "Wasim," he says, "would you like a special treat: ice cream at the store for dessert?"

"With sprinkles?" Wasim asks, and when Iskander nods, he squeals his approval. Without letting him go, not even taking him to the bathroom to wash his face, never taking another look at Zuleikha, who sits glued to her chair, Iskander leaves the house with Wasim.

Zuleikha remains sitting outside at the patio table. Should she call Patrick, warn him just in case Iskander shows up at the door? But her husband isn't one to create public scenes, and besides, he wouldn't do that with Wasim; he loves his son too much. It is Sunday, and Patrick will most certainly be with his own children, if not also with Juliet. No need to make things more complicated than they already are. And she certainly can't call her mother—it's not even dawn in Pakistan yet—to talk about any of this.

The baby starts kicking, as he has gotten into the habit of doing at regular intervals now. The curtain falls on the day, and Zuleikha's panic grows. She decides to call Iskander on his mobile, ask him to come back home, please, and bring Wasim, but when she tries to get up, she feels lightheaded and has to sit down again. Eventually she rises, discovers that she lacks the energy to carry the remnants of their dinner inside, and covers the half-empty bowls of leftover roasted cauliflower, chicken *karahi* and rice with the dirty plates. Using the walls for support, she waddles inside. The piano calls her name, as it does whenever she is alone at home, but this evening she does not answer. She goes to bed and lies down, cradling her womb.

The keys have lives of their own, they move of their own accord. She tries to tame them, but they have their own time signature. Sir Pendleton stares in icy disapproval. *If you just stop clutching your heart with your hands every time something goes wrong, and let your heart hold your hands instead, the piano will play itself.* This piano does play itself, but the music is rottenly alien. It occurs to her that what's in front of her is not a piano, but a pianola. She has always disliked video clips of them; but it's the first time she has come face to face with one. She likes it even less now.

Zuleikha is fuddled with sleep when Wasim barges into the master bedroom, his face happy and exhausted. He runs to her as if nothing has happened, starts recounting his ice cream expedition, riding his sugar high. She checks the bedside clock; they were gone for over an hour, and now it is too late for a shower because his hair won't dry before bedtime. Wasim's excitement mounts when informed of this fortuitous stroke of luck. He gambols, and she is grateful for the distraction, going through the motions as she helps him get ready for bed.

In their bedroom she finds Iskander sitting on her side of the bed, his feet dangling.

"Close the door, please," he says frostily.

She feels hideously nauseous and wants to go to the bathroom, lean over the sink and throw up, but she knows this isn't the time.

"I'll ask questions, you answer. Don't lie. Wasim told me he saw you more than once, and I hope you will not insult your son, or me, by lying."

She walks over to his side of the bed, sits down, pulls a pillow across her lap just to have something to grab on to.

"Just yes or no, please Zu. Understand?"

She starts crying. "Iskander, I don't know what I was thinking. You've given me this perfect life, too perfect, and I don't feel worthy of it sometimes..."

"Now is not the time for compliments. Yes or no—did you cheat on me?"

"I'm not trying to compliment you. What I really mean

is that I feel, have felt for a long time now, since Wasim was born, that we...I mean, I have questioned if we are worthy of each other. Because we value such different things."

Iskander wags his finger. "Zu, no more bullshit, ok? Just yes or no, please! Did you, or did you not, cheat on me?"

This most important, fundamental question she answers with silence and a hung head.

"I see." He takes a deep breath, swallows hard, clenches and unclenches his fist. His throat beats like a metronome. His stare is affixed to a point on the pillow across her stomach. There is a physical distaste in his eyes. "How many times, Zu? No—how long?"

Silence ensues. Zuleikha has imagined moments like this—despite her best efforts to block them from her mind when she was carrying on with Patrick—and wondered if there were things she could say, entreaties, promises to seek Iskander's forgiveness, and each time arrived at the conclusion that she didn't care about his forgiveness, because she did not love him. But she has never really imagined the extent of his agony when confronted with her affair. She still does not love him, but the naked anguish painted upon his face jolts her head to toe. Iskander bounces off the bed and starts pacing the room, continuing to coil and recoil his fists.

"So you've had questions about us, for this long, but instead of asking me any of those questions, you—you fuck another man?"

"Iskander, please!"

"Iskander, please? What—you're upset that I'm upset? Is that inappropriate? You commit *zina,* the punishment for which—if you did this in Pakistan—is death by stoning by the way, and I'm the one who's responding inappropriately? *Iskander, please!* Really? And then you have the gall to tell me that you've questioned if we are worthy of each other? You've questioned if I am worthy of you, you mean? What exactly is your worth, Zu? Tell me. What exactly are those piano lessons worth? Are they worth this twenty-five hundred square foot house? Where are you going?"

Zuleikha runs to the bathroom, closes the door and starts retching into the toilet. Iskander bangs on the door.

"We are going to have this discussion, Zu. If you don't come out, I am going to call your parents right now, tell them what their daughter has done. Tell them how she has treated the husband who did everything for her, her son-"

"Okay, okay. Please give me a minute."

She washes her face, scrubs it with a towel until her skin burns. When she reenters the room, Iskander stands by the bed.

"By the way, whose baby is that?" he says, pointing to her belly.

"It can't be his. We never, not once—we always used protection."

"You always, what? That's nice, isn't it? Well, fuck you!"

"Iskander? I promise you it's yours—you have to believe me."

"'Believe me!' Ha! Believe you—me? No, I can't do that! Think, Zu. This isn't a soap opera. There are ways to know, now, ways to find out. When that baby comes out, we'll all know anyway. And then," he wags his finger, "it will be too late for you to come completely clean."

Zuleikha's knees buckle. Iskander reaches for her, grabs her shoulder, it seems to steady her. But then he shakes her, and she, in turn, reaches for his shoulders and tries to shove him away.

"But you have to believe me—this is your baby," she howls.

He shakes his head. His trademark sly smile is nowhere to be found. She is still holding onto his shoulders when he takes a swing. Or perhaps, tries to slap her, she can't tell, because before she can decide what it is, she feels the impact on her neck. It makes her wince in pain. As she is falling down, she shoves him back with all her might. He staggers back against the high-canopy bed, shock on his face, and tries to get back up just as she crumples on the floor. The side of her face hits the parquet floor flush, and the impact takes the air out of her lungs. Her right ear starts ringing, she can feel her right cheek swelling like a balloon being blown, her right eye shutting. Both eyes closed, she tries to turn on her back. She doesn't see what happens next. She doesn't see, doesn't know, whether Iskander slips and falls on her, or deliberately jumps on her and stomps on her belly. All she feels is the heel of his shoe, the weight of his body, fall on her belly like an anvil. The pain sears through her and a scream forms in her mouth, but it doesn't escape it, for there is no air left in her. Her eyes bulge open with shock, the lavender wall of the bedroom turns white in a flash. She tries to reach for her belly, but now Iskander is on top of her, a pile of arms and legs and flesh. Her hands have no feeling in them; they seem like someone else's hands, they seem made of plastic, of rubber. They lack the strength to push him off. Her eyes squeeze shut again and she grits her teeth in anguish.

Finally he rolls off her, but then he gives a guttural groan. The groan turns into an incoherent whimper. When those insensate hands of hers that feel as if they belong to someone else find her own skin, they discover the shape of the baby that was supposed to be safely inside her now pushing very tightly against her skin, almost protruding out of her stomach. She gasps, forces herself to open her good eye. An obscure shape of the fetus is, indeed, pressing out.

Iskander yelps, "Oh my God, my God! Zu! I'm sorry! Allahu Akbar. Allahu Akbar."

She tries to push the fetus back into the womb, where it is supposed to belong. Then it occurs to her that by doing so, she might be doing more harm than is already done. The smell becomes terrible. Iskander is vomiting next to her on the floor. "Help," she says.

He looks up, immediately his eyes go to her belly. He points at it with the ghastliness of a wretched ghost. "I'm sorry! Forgive me," he says, and starts vomiting again. His vomit falls next to her, on her, in acidic, half-chewed chunks of the remains of her cooking.

"Get me help. Call the ambulance," she begs again.

He tries to get up, but can't get back up. He starts crawling, banging his head on the floor once as if under siege of an extravagant rapture.

She bends her head to watch him reach the door, where he pulls himself up by grabbing the doorknob. She hears him on the phone. Her body feels as if it is wrapped in coil. She realizes she is bleeding. Blood is soaking the space between her legs. Or maybe it isn't blood. Does blood smell like that? Could it be something else? Amniotic fluid? She doesn't know. She wants to know, she wants

Iskander to tell her because she cannot move. "Look," she wants to tell him, "He looks just like you. That head looks just like yours."

Iskander does not come back inside. Her voice has left her. She cannot call him. Her hands hold the shape of the fetus, it doesn't move. But then, the baby is crying. That is good. That means the baby has life. They are going to call him Zafar. Wasim is going to show his little brother Zafar his way around the play structure in the park, how to kick the ball, how to douse ice cream with sprinkles and gobble it up. Zafar is crying louder now. Zafar is screaming. But how can an unborn fetus scream? She realizes it is not Zafar, but the siren. The wailing gets louder and louder, before it stops. Zafar stops. But he already stopped. He didn't exist. But he did. He is still.

For the next few moments, the world, the entire Milky Way, is perfectly still. Out of that stillness a memory emerges, a vision from a childhood visit to her grandparents'. A crowd is gathered. They are facing a wall. A stoning is about to take place. Her mother grabs Zuleikha's hand and crosses the street, starts pulling her away from the scene. Who, why, doesn't matter. Zuleikha is nine. Mamajaan isn't going to let her witness a person being stoned to death. "Allahu Akbar," she mumbles. Someone is banging on the door. Zuleikha feels tied down, facing a perverted pile of people. The Milky Way collapses around her like a black hole. Loud knocks on the door feel like rocks being hurled at her. Her parents married her off and sent her to America, and still someone is throwing rocks at her.

She has one foot in a dream, the other in a daze. She is

on a gurney. Her legs are pulled apart and she is open to the world. It is bright as day, but dark as night. Her skin feels so cold as if it has frozen into a sheet of ice, while inside her, the flame of God burns, hot enough to melt her bones. Faces covered by masks hover on both sides. She feels sticks of dynamite inserted into her cervix, ready to detonate. She has cramps like she never had with Wasim, even during those final frantic pushes to get him out. A giant storm forms inside her, builds momentum; she has never seen a tornado up close, only on television, but one is inside her now, its funnel cloud churning, flipping whatever lies in its path, and it circles little Zafar. Her baby tries to crawl away from it. His heart beats faster...or is that the beating of her own heart? Both hearts beat faster, like off-beats being pounded on the massive bass drums of a marching band. The tornado engulfs Zafar, tosses him around like a hapless, fallen branch. Zafar lies limp in the tornado's wake. Something, someone, tries to pull at Zafar, but he doesn't move. Giant forceps—or is that a crane?—try this way and that for a better grip, tug at Zafar, yank him out. Now a broom is sweeping the tornado's debris, gathering it in piles, then a giant contraption appears out of nowhere in her belly. It is vacuuming her insides. She can't see it, but she can visualize it: it's a comical apparatus, like the Whatchamajigger of the Cat in the Hat, but it performs no comic act. It sucks her dry.

When she opens her eyes, her mother sits next to the bed. A monitor attached to a stand beeps a slow tempo next to her, and a boxy machine beyond the stand buzzes a dull aural humdrum. Sunlight is sliced into thin white-gold strips by the window blinds. A voice on the intercom is announcing something outside the room. Her mother reaches forward and holds her hand, but Zuleikha lacks the strength to squeeze back. Her hand lies etiolated in her mother's. She remembers her mother's abiding approach to difficult situations, and a flicker of fear flows through her.

"I'm still your *Beti*, aren't I, Mamajaan?" she asks her mother. "Can you forgive me?"

"There's nothing to forgive, dear. Shh!" Mamajaan says. She remains uncharacteristically serene, and for that, Zuleikha is senselessly grateful.

The next time she wakes up, Mamajaan has metamorphosed into a bespectacled, bouffanted woman who looks nothing like the one who brought her into the world. The stranger holds Zuleikha's gaping stare in an unembarrassed gaze of appraisal, so lengthy as to be almost ill-mannered, before she speaks.

"Let's try this again," the woman says. "Wasim is with me. Your son is safe, he is fine. That's the first thing you need to know. My staff is specially trained to make him feel at home. Second—I'm taking you with me too. Not right now, not today, maybe not even tomorrow. But when you are ready to be released, you're coming with me. I'll take care of the two of you. And third: in case you're wondering, my name's Reza. I run the Oasis Foundation. It's a shelter for Muslim women and children. Someone at the police department referred you to me. That's all you need to know for now. No, no; no need to speak. Just nod if you understand what I said."

"Zafar," Zuleikha whispers.

"He is with us, dear. Your son is safe."

"Zafar?"

"I'm sorry, I thought his name was Iskander? It's okay, he won't find you, I promise. There's a protective order in place and he doesn't know where you are and where your son is. But I can see you're tired—all those drugs! It's okay; I'll be here. We'll talk again when you're feeling better."

"Zafar?" Zuleikha asks again.

The woman continues to look at her quizzically, until a realization spreads across her face like the first array of daylight across dark, sodden earth. "Oh! Zafar. Oh, I see," she murmurs, and now she reaches for Zuleikha's hand, squeezes it gently. The woman purses her lips together and does not say anything else. She continues to look straight into Zuleikha.

: PART II :

Wasim lets go of her hand just before they reach the children's playroom at the shelter, and it irks Zuleikha. She remembers how shy her son used to be when she first started taking him to his daycare. Wasim would cling to her, hesitant to break the chain link between his little fist and hers, and seek the comfort of her voice and the reassurance of her answer by asking repeatedly when she was coming back to pick him up. Now he carries on with the air of someone who is not only more familiar with their new dwelling than she is (which is true, since he has, indeed, been there several days longer), but also a boy who has acquired a heaping helping of animal nous and aged a lot more than the week—a year, perhaps—he has had to live alone without his parents.

She reaches for his shoulder and gently holds him back, leans in front of him and says, "You don't want to say bye to your Mamajaan?"

Wasim steals a calculating glance in the direction of the other kids in the playroom, and Zuleikha's eyes follow his. The room is painted a festive yellow, a rainbow arching across the long side wall. Near the front, a young attendant sits on a wooden armchair, rocking a baby with a bottle, while a toddler crawls around nearby. Past them, a mite of boys and girls grouped by gender play boisterously, while further back, a smaller boy sits quietly on a chair, ignoring the play, reading, utterly self-possessed and unfathomably inscrutable. Next to him sits another attendant, an older woman in a *burkha* wearing an expression of primness, keeping a watchful eye on the proceedings.

"Mamajaan!" Wasim mutters in protest, and Zuleikha flushes, conscious only of the urge to throw her arms around him again. She has smothered him since being reunited with him the previous evening. Wasim's face assumes an expression of consternation, as if he can see right through her, and she realizes that if she does what her heart desires she stands only to embarrass her son, and gain further distance from him in return.

"I'll see you at lunch, okay?" she says, ignoring the pang of anguish that pricks her heart. She gives him a gentle pat on the shoulder, urging him on. Relief washes across Wasim's face. He turns around, takes off his shoes and places them in the bin by the door, and makes his way to the pack in the back.

From the children's playroom, Zuleikha walks across the narrow corridor with dark carpet and whitewashed walls, past the reception desk and the row of administrative offices—including Reza's—none yet open. Upon reaching the family room at the other end of the corridor, she hears someone weeping.

A woman sits crumpled on a chair, surrounded by several others—standing, hovering over her. A pair of women kneel by her, one of them rubbing her knee affectionately, while a middle-aged, corpulent woman in a bright red t-shirt and ash-colored sweatpants sits in the chair next to her, an arm around the crying woman's shoulder.

The woman in the red t-shirt says, "You miss him. We all do. But it go away. Listen to me: it go away."

"You not understand, Yusra," the other woman says discomposedly. "I was sad after the lawyer. I tell *jihal* we take vote. Massii and Mohamed say yes. Me and Sofia? We say no. We not want to go back home. Then Massii say, 'What about Abbi's vote? If Abbi here, Abbi vote yes, I know. Then it's three-two. We win.' Like football. Sofia say, 'No. I like it here. Ommee's happy here.' Then Massii hit Sofia. Hit her neck, just like his Abbi hit me. Make Sofia cry. Now I not know what to do."

Zuleikha feels, as one does when accidentally stumbling upon the climactic scene of an unfamiliar soap opera episode, guiltily voyeuristic, unable to look away. Hardback plastic chairs are strewn haphazardly across the room, and she finds one a little farther away from the group and sits down. Her slight movements and noise cause the other women to turn. She forms what she hopes is a sympathetic, solemn hint of a smile on her face, but they pay no mind to her and turn their attention back to the crying woman. An older woman starts to speak in Farsi, but Yusra's voice carries over hers.

"And you want to go back to that, Atifah?" she says, patting the young woman on the shoulder. "You say he beat. He show knife. You say you scared for him, you scared for all family. He give you no money, not let you call home. You cook, he eat. The *jihal* eat. You not eat. He not even tell you nine-one-one what is. Now your *jihal* hit like he, just like my *jihal*. If you go back, you learn to hit. How I learn to hit, I not take any more hit so I hit back. Then you come back here again, you and I fight. If you live, and come back here, we fight. Fight is all we do with our lives."

The other women nod in agreement, make short exclamations of assent. One shivers exaggeratedly as if struck by a sudden chill. Zuleikha tries to guess Atifah's age, but can't. The woman wears a bright blue Sana'ani curtain-style dress, and her face—except for her tear-stained eyes—are covered by a black Al-Momq face-cover, with Arabic inscriptions colored red and white. Now she pulls the Al-Momq over those eyes, and her body is racked by a torrent of tears.

Dr. Reza Yousef appears at the door. She lingers for a long moment on the threshold, a benevolent smile upon her lips. Her eyes hover over each face, including Zuleikha's, in unembarrassed looks of appraisal, and once again it occurs to Zuleikha that Reza might be one of those rare souls that never feels the need to resort to subterfuge, or search for a lost temper. The director of the shelter motions the other women to sit down. The women surrounding Atifah disperse and take chairs, while Reza takes Yusra's vacated spot next to the aqueous mess that is Atifah, who immediately places her head on Reza's lap like a distraught child.

"Is Allah's destiny for me, Reza," Atifah says, her voice a hoarse whisper. "Lawyer say criminal court hard to prove if *jihal* not testify. Mohamed not know what happen, Sofia not know what happen, not see anything. She five year, Reza. Five! Mohamed—three. Now Massii, he know what happen. But he love his Abbi. He not say any bad thing about Abbi. So is his Abbi's word and my word. Who judge believe? But in family court their Abbi get visit...ation. He even get *jihal*, because he make money, I not make any money. That's what lawyer say. One way or another, I face him. Have to. Not today, not tomorrow, but someday. I not escape. So I think. I think I go back to Iraq, ask judge. But lawyer say the judge not say yes. And if *jihal* go to Iraq, what they see then? No. It better go back to him, the most thing is make *jihal* happy."

"Let me recite you a poem," Reza says, stroking Atifah's hair.

A collective groan escapes from the group of other women.

"Reza, this real problem, Atifah's!" Yusra says in a warning tone. "Last night Huda see her in lobby, two at night. She on the phone with he."

"That *is* a real problem, and now you know why we don't have phones in the rooms. It's why, if you *have* cell phones, I ask you to never answer when he calls or texts you. Once you start the conversation, he'll say sorry, act nice, and it will become that much harder to get back on your own feet. But you know what? We have a lot of real problems. And we'll get to them in a minute, but before that—just listen! This is a short one, and it applies to all of us here, even though it's a thousand years old."

Reza recites a verse in Farsi, and only the older woman in the group nods as if she understands, while the rest look on as if in a trance. Zuleikha can only make out a word or two, yet she is struck by the melody of Reza's voice.

"Our treasure. The world's treasure. Which is why an Englishman wanted to translate it, so the rest of the world could also read our Omar Khayyám," Reza continues.

"'There was a Door to which I found no Key
There was a Veil past which I could not see
Some little Talk awhile of Me and Thee
There seemed—and then no more of Thee and Me.'

"We made it through the stone ages," Reza says, "and

we are still going to make it through this age too, because they can't live without us. If we're gone, they're gone. Now that might make you feel as if you're nothing but a womb, but you—all of you—helped write Tanweer's college application last week, and I know you all know about Fatima's custody extension. Look at all that and tell me whether you think there's hope."

Zuleikha feels a lump in her throat. She looks around, sees another woman in a burnt orange *kaftan* dabbing her eyes, but Atifah has now stopped crying. In the hush stillness of the room, Reza's voice sounds like that of an enchantress come to cast a spell.

"So yes, we'll talk about Atifah's meeting with the lawyer. There are options to think about. Intessar has an immigration hearing coming up—that's exciting, and I want someone to be the menu coordinator for the big *al Mi'raj* dinner in May. It's on a Saturday this year and all of our trustees, board members and major donors will be here, so it's a big deal. But before we do all that, let's meet our new neighbor, Zuleikha."

The room falls silent for a long moment.

Then Yusra says, pointing to the television mounted at a corner of the room, "We know who is she. We know what she done."

None of the women turn around and greet Zuleikha.

"I hope you'll not make too big a deal of their behavior today," Reza says to Zuleikha after all the other women have left the room. "They'll warm up to you, and when that happens, they'll become very protective, especially that Yusra, mark my words. It's just that they're not used to seeing one of their own leading off the local news two nights in a row. In any case, I'll have a word with them."

"Please don't. It'll only make it worse. I think I get it. They don't think I'm a victim."

A hint of a smile appears on the corners of Reza's lips.

"I always wanted to play an instrument. How did you get interested in the piano?"

Zuleikha tells Reza about her Papajaan's bootleg collection of Ahmad Jamal records and his perpetual fascination with a man born Baptist in Pennsylvania turning to Allah for the eternal salvation of his soul. They continue to talk awhile of commonplace matters, and Zuleikha is grateful for the distraction of chit chat. Reza gets up and opens the window blinds, flooding the family room with sunlight, before walking across and straightening the arras hanging from the wall, tenderly running her fingers along the tapestry's resplendent brown stallions with their intricately sewn milky-white stockings.

"A gift—someone who wishes to remain anonymous donated this from his private collection when we opened the shelter," she tells Zuleikha. "Hand stitched by Yoruk bride-girls in some Karaviran village at the nook of the mountain of Hassan. I can't tell you how many times I've wondered if I can find another rich collector to buy it from us at a fair price. But then, I think, all these rich people know each other, right? How would it look if the buyer invited the donor to a party and, well, you know! That just wouldn't look right."

"You would make a fine piano player with those long fingers," Zuleikha says.

"Thank you, dear." Reza pulls up a chair and sits across Zuleikha, their knees grazing. "But do you want to know why I've thought of selling it? People like Atifah have been treated their entire lives like those bride-girls. They come from places where even if they find a way to go to the police, the police will turn around and bring them right back home. You know places like that, don't you? Then they arrive at this country by marriage, they think they'll be free from the lives of their mothers and grandmothers, and instead, they are told, 'You're mine, I can do with you whatever I want.' Do you know what I am talking about?"

For the first time Zuleikha feels uncomfortable in Reza's presence. Her mind boggles a bit as she silently observes the pleasant lady who amiably asks her these questions. Reza is nowhere near as old as her mother, maybe not even fifty, she thinks—an observation that makes her shudder at the thought of how drugged up and disoriented she must have been at the hospital to have confused one with the other. The few wrinkles on Reza's face, if anything, add a layer of bearing and assurance, lest anyone confuses her candor and mischievous demeanor with youth.

"Until that girl Aasiya got beheaded by her estranged husband up in Buffalo New York, nobody even acknowledged that this was a problem for Muslim women in this country. I went to mosques, parties, restaurants and businesses asking for help, and all I heard were two things: 'No,' and, 'You got a Ph.D. for *that*?' I showed them pictures of shards of glass stuck in the back of one woman after her husband pushed her through a table. They didn't want to see them. So if one of our girls somehow got past the myth that men are superior and violence is permitted, somehow decided to risk being tarred a prostitute for standing up to her husband, was somehow intrepid enough to call the police, what do you think happened? She ended up in a shelter that served pork and had no prayer room. That's like trying to save the skin on your back by agreeing to let someone break your backbone instead.

"The reason I'm telling you this, Zuleikha, is that I think you'll agree your situation is different from the other women's. And they have heard the statements made by your husband's lawyer on the evening news; they've seen the newspaper stories. They may not have understood everything, but they understood just enough to form their own opinions. You were everywhere for a few days last week. So you'll forgive them for being resentful and acting a little boorish, won't you?"

"Of course," Zuleikha says, caught unaware and feeling embarrassed. "A nurse at the hospital mentioned the news once, but I had no idea all of this was going on."

"Not your fault, dear, and I know you will. Which brings me to the other thing I want to talk about," Reza replies.

Zuleikha is vaguely aware of another quality hidden beneath the layers of compassion and grace, mischief and friendship in Reza's personality, but she cannot quite put her finger on what it is.

Reza leans in close, pats Zuleikha on the knee and says, "Some of our money comes from various foundations, but we also have these individual donors, Zuleikha, that have standing in the community. They want to help women and children in need, but they are all also concerned about protecting the image of Muslims in general; surely you can understand why, can't you?" She waits for Zuleikha to nod in agreement before continuing. "They have other vested interests. Some, for example, are involved with setting up an Islamic Tribunal right here in North Texas, so that we Muslims can settle our disputes cheaply, according to our customs and laws. And so I've been asked to set up a meeting between you and a couple of the gentlemen involved with this tribunal. They think they can help with your situation. I'll go with you; they can't come here. They're not supposed to know the exact location of our shelter, even though I suspect that they do. Just like the media, who have been calling me every day to see if they can get five minutes with you. I've said no to them, of course! But I can't say no to this meeting, dear."

"I see. When is this meeting supposed to take place?"

"Only when you're feeling strong enough. But the sooner the better; isn't that how it always is with these things? Same with the police investigators, and let me tell you: they're *really* anxious to get hold of you. So if you're up for it, why don't we get this informal tribunal get-together out of the way? Tomorrow? Your husband is out on bail and already lawyered-up, as they say. There's an automatic sixty-one-day protective order—what's called an ex-parte—prohibiting him from contacting you, but here we are already a week into it. You have many decisions to make, but don't worry. You'll not have to do anything you don't want to do. Remember, I'll always have your back. But today...why don't you just spend time with your son and rest? Also, think about what you want to make for the big dinner. Do you have a signature dish, something to really impress your new neighbors?"

Wasim sits at the small desk in the corner of their second-story room which the functional furniture fits to a miracle, while Zuleikha leans against the pillow on the bed, sipping tepid tea, her abstracted eyes half-focused on her son engrossed in his drawing, and half-resting, past him—through the window and across the interstate—upon the shadowy silhouette of the high-rise hotel in the distance, where she occasionally met Patrick. She attempts, in vain, to impose some semblance of order to the wildly divergent feelings in her heart, surprised and perturbed with herself that memories of Patrick still move her, despite not having seen him in months and all that has happened since. But when she tries to block out thoughts of him, she finds herself transported to another world situated at a strange confluence of time and space, one in which an online newspaper story, accompanied by a mugshot of Iskander, rests under the headline:

IRVING MAN ACCUSED OF CAUSING MISCARRIAGE COULD FACE FETICIDE CHARGES

Earlier that afternoon, that picture, with the look of distress and utter disbelief in the half-closed eyes, had made Zuleikha cringe. The headline she had found grossly tawdry, and, feeling other eyes upon her in the cramped computer room next to the family room downstairs, she'd been unable to read further. She had logged into her email account instead. There were notifications of specials from the online toys-and-clothing store for babies; she had bit her lip while unsubscribing from them, and ignored the notes from two of her three remaining students wondering about missed appointments, as well as an "Urgent!" inquiry from Heath, no doubt also about her delinquency and unknown whereabouts. There was a circular from the New Mexico Music Academy in Albuquerque about a special summer learning program on the Lescetizky method of teaching by a renowned Russian piano professor. Out of morbid curiosity more than anything else, Zuleikha had clicked on that email. Lescetizky himself had taught some all-time greats, and the academy's website made mention of the marvelous opportunities that opened up for those who successfully completed the program, but admission was competitive, and to qualify, one had to submit a portfolio of your work, already have some teaching experience, and arrange for an original copy of their music diploma sent directly to the academy, along with two letters of recommendation.

She had given a ghost of a chuckle, closing the email. That was when she noticed the note from Patrick, with the subject line: "Zuleikha! Are you ok??? Please respond, PLEASE!" Other than to confirm lesson schedules, they had never exchanged emails before. In a fit of panic she had closed the browser, logged off from the computer, and gone across the hallway to retrieve Wasim.

During dinner, Wasim had wanted to sit next to two other boys and she had let him, despite her own desires. She'd walked with her tray and sat down next to the older woman she had seen earlier, forcing a smile and introducing herself, but it turned out that this woman, apart from telling Zuleikha her name, Huda, and country of origin, Yemen, could say nothing else except in Arabic, a language Zuleikha didn't understand, and so the two had continued to sit side by side ruminatively and finish their meal in silence, exchanging nothing but awkward glances and smiles every once in a while.

Now she searches desperately for something to feel grateful about and finds but a little. The room, bereft of the accumulations resulting from longer occupation, habits, traditions, and individual quirks, feels hollow, and so does her mind. She is glad that neither she nor Iskander maintained a social media presence, that they are both introverts floating outside the bubbles of expansive networks. But then Zuleikha can't help but wonder if having other friends, or being more active in the mosque, might have brought her and Iskander closer and given their marriage more of a chance to flourish, or at the very least, somehow stopped her from getting entangled with Patrick. That name—again! She forces herself to tear away from it, remembers that she didn't see any email from her brother Jameel. Communication with him has been mostly one sided, with her checking up on him from time to time, but if he had an inkling about what has happened, surely he would have tried to contact her. It occurs to her that not even a fortnight has passed since she last called home and spoke with her parents, and therefore it is unlikely that her family in Pakistan is even suspicious of anything amiss. She can simply call them this weekend and say she suffered a miscarriage, and no one would be wiser. That line of thinking finally puts her mind in a bit of ease, and she makes a mental note to ask Reza how she can go about making international calls from the shelter.

Wasim gets up from the desk and comes to her, hands her the picture he has been drawing. She'd observed him scrubbing furiously on the page earlier, and now she sees the outcome of her son's efforts: a stick house with a chimney against an ominous brownish-yellow back-ground; two windows and a door, a yard with black grass on the front and a pathway cutting across the middle. Stick mother and child on one side of that pathway, father on the other.

"You miss Papajaan, don't you, *Beta*?"

"He doesn't know how to cook, Mamajaan! He is afraid of the kitchen."

She pulls him up close and tries to lean back, but just like his father, the boy refuses to go to bed until he has changed into his pajamas. So she waits until he gets ready. Eyes shiny, he finally approaches with trepidation the bed the two are to share. This time, he doesn't protest when she beckons him. He lies on top of her and she pulls the blanket atop him, making herself small by lifting her knees up. Within a few minutes, he slumbers peacefully. She turns slightly so that they are side by side and she is no longer stifled under his weight.

Somewhere outside, a woman starts whimpering and thumping on the wall. Zuleikha hears a door open and Yusra's voice call out, berating the crying woman, but the whimpering does not stop.

Pulling into the parking lot the next day, Reza says, "Those donation box clothes look good on you, but I bet you can't wait until tomorrow."

"Well, I'm looking forward to getting some of our stuff," Zuleikha replies, "but I wouldn't call it 'can't wait.' More like very nervous, even though Iskander won't be there. Thank you for agreeing to go with me instead of sending someone else along."

She's been going over the list in her mind: Wasim's toys, books, and his blanket, her music books and CDs, including the handful of her own recordings—those are the must haves. Then the clothes—whatever she can fit into the trunk of her car and Reza's. But the car is the most important thing. Her own transportation!

Ahead of them, the tilt-wall, massive *Masjid* rises across the street from a municipal golf course like something out of an animated epic, glossy white with green and tinted glass. At the lobby, they are met by a receptionist. He is a scrawny man in his twenties wearing a pair of slacks and a shirt both too large for him. He checks off their names on a list, then walks them past the enormous windows looking into the gymnasium—where a basketball game and a volleyball match are simultaneously taking place on opposite ends—all the way down to the other end of the long hallway and into a small conference room.

"Did someone ask you to take us to the only room in this building with no windows?" Reza asks the man with a malevolent smile. The man stares back at her blankly as if she might as well be speaking in Latin. He leaves, comes back with a pitcher of water and glasses and sets them on the table, then leaves again.

They wait awhile. One of the games going on at the gym reaches fever pitch and some sort of argument breaks out. Voices are raised and a whistle blows shrilly. Then two men enter the conference room. The taller of the two is dressed in a business suit and has thinning white hair, an aristocratic nose and a sweet smile. He walks over to them and shakes their hands, introducing himself as Selim Burakgazi, a member of the mosque's board, and apologizing for keeping them waiting.

In a wicked manner, as if she and Selim Burakgazi are old acquaintances engaged in nothing more than the newest episode of bantering rivalry in a long-running situation comedy, Reza says, "I must protest, Mr. Burakgazi, on account that the Masjid makes a lofty promise of majesty from the outside, and then we are shown into a room that's only fit to be the maids' quarters."

"I assure you it has nothing to do with the fact that you are women," Mr. Burakgazi replies. He wears a tranquil smile that suggests a regal breeding of countless centuries. "Until yesterday we weren't sure you were coming, and they have a lot going on here every day, as you can see. And normally I'd have asked you to meet at my office which is just a mile east of the High-5 Interchange, but this man simply doesn't have the time to get away from here, even for lunch. But who are we to complain about his availability? If he hadn't agreed to leave London and move here, we'd still be praying at the *musalla,* struggling to raise funds for this place. Instead, here we are. Thirty-two hundred prayer spaces ready for Ramadan this year, Insaah'Allah. Please allow me to introduce Imam Jaloliddin Sheikh."

Mr. Burakgazi points to his companion who has no mustache but a long beard, a pair of large, intelligent eyes, and a heavy jowl. The Imam wears stylish, wire-rimmed round glasses, a bright orange and red *chapan* tied with a kerchief at the waist, and a *tubeteika* perched atop his jet-black hair. He acknowledges the two women with slight nods and a thin smile. He sits across from them and spreads out a thick black folder and a pair of books—one of them the Quran, with leather filigree bindings—on the desk in front of him.

Taking a chair next to Imam Jaloliddin, Mr. Burakgazi

says, "There's been so much interest in this case already. Now am I correct in assuming that you haven't already met with anyone from the DA's office?"

"That's right," Reza replies. "I have done what was asked of me, which was to get her to talk to you first."

"Thank you. We appreciate that. I don't know how much Dr. Yousef has had a chance to tell you about us, Mrs. Khan, so forgive me if you've already heard anything I have to say."

Imam Jaloliddin gives an impatient shrug. The gesture does not escape Dr. Burakgazi's attention, but it does not cause him to lose touch with his smile.

"Let me just start here: you know how lawyers aren't cheap, right? They charge hundreds per hour; good living if you can make it," he laughs. "So if a couple can't agree to disagree in a civil way, their divorce can easily cost them the college education of a child. The same goes for two brothers fighting over an inheritance. And the courts in this country are clogged enough as it is; which brings us to our tribunal, where all we're trying to do is resolve disputes cheaply and amicably, have a full panel of four respected and experienced Imams like this wise gentleman here review the case for—let's say—a few hundred dollars at most, and issue a ruling that not only follows state law, but is also Shariah compliant.

"But as soon as word gets out that we Muslims are doing what the Jews have been doing in their *beth dins* forever, how the Catholics do their marriage annulments in their diocesan tribunals, there's a Texas Congressman introducing a bill against foreign laws taking over the land. But now there's talk of this...this stealth jihad on the American court system. The Jews have their path to walk upon—their Halakhah; no one cares. We have our path to water, except we call it Shariah, and everybody is up in arms. Now I don't have to tell you, Mrs. Khan, that Shariah is a lot more than maiming and stoning. And it might interest you to know that our scholars in the holy land are debating and trying to modify those corporal punishments even as we speak. But people here act as if it's just us Muslims, as if there has never been any harsh punishment in Judeo-Christian history. They act like Deuteronomy does not exist. We have a state representative asking any Muslim who enters her office to pledge allegiance to America and renounce terrorism, as if we've all somehow embraced it before. Now you have the mayor of your town going on right-wing shows and accusing us of trying to bypass American laws, when we clearly state on our website that we are nothing but a mediation and nonbinding arbitration firm. She is holding hearings to whip up her base by denigrating us; she's putting her council on the spot to support this discriminatory bill."

"Forgive me," Reza interjects, "but you are not running for a seat somewhere, are you, and this is not a political debate, is it? I don't see a stage and am sorry, but this is hardly the time to lecture us, especially this young woman."

Zuleikha tries to think of something sensible to say, but acutely aware of the cold stare of Imam Jaloliddin's eyes upon her, she finds herself wordless. She is grateful for Reza's presence next to her. If it weren't for the gravity of the situation she finds herself in, she thinks, she'd find this conversation no more than a mild curiosity and follow it with faint amusement. She has never been the type to be interested in the latest happenings of the real world out there—as Iskander liked to call it. She takes a deep breath and tries to concentrate.

"Two things, Dr. Yousef. First and foremost, our objective today is to assess the situation, hear Mrs. Khan out and see what advice the Imam has for her, and determine what's best for this family and how to navigate this horrible legal mess it is in. But there's something else. Now obviously, we'd all like to see the family—just as we'd like to see any other family—weather its storms and stick together, but if Mrs. Khan decides further down the road that a divorce is the best way to move forward, then I'm here to inform her that we can set up a tribunal hearing and reach an amicable agreement that is a lot cheaper than outside lawyers."

"You just did; thank you. I'd just like to remind you she is still recovering from a traumatic experience."

"And that is all because of what she did, isn't it?" Imam Jaloliddin says in a peculiar accent that is hard to pinpoint but carries English undertones, pointing his finger at Zuleikha, startling her. The Imam affixes an incalculable gaze upon her through his glasses and now addresses her directly.

"Excuse me, young lady. Your husband says he loved you, he never mistreated you, he loves your son, and he gave the two of you everything you needed. Do you agree?"

Zuleikha finds her breath caught by a strange terror. She can only nod in response.

"So despite all of those blessings, you committed *zina* with a *shirk*. A *shirk* who is married and who, even if he wasn't married, you can never marry unless he declares his Islam and adheres to Islamic rulings, because it is not permissible for a Muslim woman to be the wife of a disbeliever. This is a matter on which those scholars that Mr. Burakgazi spoke about all agree. If you wish, I shall have copies made for you of the relevant passages from *al-Mumtahinah* and *al-Baqarah*.

"Furthermore, instead of confessing your sin and asking for forgiveness, instead of giving your husband and your mosque a chance to condone your offenses, you continued to live like an unregenerate. Until you got caught, that is. Then you argued and pushed each other—something that's quite common among husbands and wives—and he fell on you by accident. What happened after that is tragic and sad. We all agree. But you can't deny that the events that led to it are your fault, and yours alone, can you?"

Reza interrupts with a biting tone unfamiliar to Zuleikha. "Forgive me, Imam; I don't think it's as simple as you make it sound. We don't know if it was by accident. That may be her husband's version of events—"

"Okay," the Imam retorts. "Let's let the young lady speak for herself and listen to her version of the events and divine this undivine riddle once and for all." Never taking his eyes off Zuleikha, he uses the end of the kerchief tied around his waist to wipe his forehead. "Why don't *you* tell us what happened?"

Zuleikha feels choking sobs rising up her throat. "I'd like to go to the restroom. May I?" she asks.

"You don't need anybody's permission to go to the restroom!" Reza says sharply. "Just go! Do you know where it is?"

She nods and escapes. In front of the mirror, she takes deep breaths and tries to compose herself and her thoughts so that she can speak succinctly upon her return.

But that seems impossible. She has half a mind to not go back inside that room. She wouldn't, if only Reza was still not in there.

Outside the restroom, Zuleikha pauses by the windows looking into the gym. The volleyball game is still going on, but the basketball game has ended. Only one youngster, a curly-haired teenage boy, runs around the court all by himself, dribbling the ball, arching this way and that to shoot from various angles.

Did Imam Jaloliddin ever do anything for fun, she wonders. Or was he always the solitary, studious type, memorizing his Quran in some quiet corner of his Madrasa? She tries to picture the Imam as a young man, running around on a field somewhere, but can't. Instead, the image that forms itself, suddenly and out of nowhere, is that of her own son, hitting a tennis ball against a wall. Wasim wears the same look of utter concentration as he administers a brutish beating upon the ball, again and again, forehand, backhand, but not to a partner. Only to a wall. He does not have a brother to play with.

She grimaces. *I must think of something else.*

Sometimes, when she was much younger and obsessed with her instrument, she would imagine what it would be like to play in front of a thousand people in an auditorium. In those days, she never asked herself how this event would come about, or why anybody else besides her own father, brother, and possibly her mother, would have any use for it. She'd play Grieg's Concerto, of course. The third movement was always her favorite, not the more famous introduction. Every bar of that piece she'd practice then like the boy now practices his shots.

Again, she makes a face. *I can't think about this. Not*

now, I mustn't.

"Zuleikha! You all right?"

She turns to see Reza with her head poking out of the door to the conference room.

Without waiting for Zuleikha to respond, Reza steps outside and walks up to her. "Are you all right?" she asks again.

"I was just watching that boy, remembering this dream I used to have when I was that age."

"In other words, you're daydreaming about a daydream. Oh, Zuleikha," Reza says disapprovingly.

"I'm sorry, Reza. It's just that—I don't think I want to go back inside that room."

"I understand. But listen to me—just do me this one favor. I'm sorry I agreed to this, but I really owe it to them. So here's what you do: everything they ask, answer yes, no, or I don't know or I can't remember or I need to think about that and get back to you. That's it. Can you do that?"

Zuleikha nods. Her feet feel heavy as together they walk back and reenter the room. Dr. Burakgazi and Imam Jaloliddin stop talking.

"I'm sorry, Madams," the Imam says impatiently. "But as I was telling this gentleman here, I have prayers coming up and a lot else to do. So why don't we pick back up where we left off and you—Mrs. Khan—tell us exactly what happened that night?"

Zuleikha says feebly, "I couldn't see. Everything happened so fast."

Imam Jaloliddin exaggeratedly shrugs his shoulders. "She doesn't know what happened. She's not disagreeing with what her husband says, mind you! She's just admitting that she doesn't know what happened.

Everything happened so fast; well of course they did! Her husband—whose family, colleagues and even boss, a boss who's not Muslim, by the way, all agree is a decent, hardworking man; they all say he's never been caught in a lie—on the other hand swears he fell on her by accident."

All the control she's been trying to muster disappears in a blink, and Zuleikha loses her battle with the sobs. Reza pulls her chair closer to hers and hands her a pack of tissues.

Blowing her nose into one, Zuleikha whispers, "I feel like I'm in a dream."

"On that point, I agree," the Imam counters, a triumphant gleam in his eyes behind those statement-making glasses. Droplets of sweat have formed on his forehead again, and this time he wipes them off with the back of his arm. "I'm afraid you've been daydreaming for a long time, young lady. That's what led to all this; not anything your husband did. And now we have reached this point where he is facing a long prison sentence, he is being vilified as a baby-killer. He has already been convicted in the court of public opinion, when he almost certainly looked forward to that new baby more than you did. He has been sundered from the son that he misses more than anything else, because there is a court order preventing him from seeing him. He doesn't know where his son is sleeping at night, what he is eating, doing. He is worried sick on top of being worried sick. Does that sound fair to you?"

Mr. Burakgazi discreetly clears his throat and interjects. "Mrs. Khan, we've been put in touch with Mr. Khan by intermediaries at the Irving mosque. Now it's important to point out that we are not speaking on your husband's behalf, nor has he asked us to say anything to you; he's forbidden from contacting you, even through third parties. But he has indicated—and his attorney has issued public statements to this effect—that he would like nothing better than to have his family back together the way it was before. He's thinking of his family, and that's noble, don't you think? Because it's not just his fate at stake here, but yours and your son's as well. I daresay that what happens in this case will also have an impact on the image of the entire Muslim community, and not just here but nationwide—"

"Can we please not put any more pressure on this woman than she is already facing? And dispense with this good-cop bad-cop routine?" Reza says in a shrill voice. She puts her arm around Zuleikha's shoulder. "Do you want some water, dear?" She proceeds to pour her a cup without waiting for a response. "Is there any way to turn the temperature down in this room?"

"Of course," replies Mr. Burakgazi, getting up from the chair and walking over to the thermostat.

"Yes, let us please dispense with this good-cop routine," Imam Jaloliddin says, shaking his head with displeasure. He continues to stare right through Zuleikha.

"Niceties will accomplish nothing here. What you need is a dose of reality. May I remind you what would happen if you did what you did in your home country?" He digs through his Quran, continues, "Here's what the *an-Noor* has to say about it: 'In the case of a previously married man committing *zina* with a previously married woman, the punishment is one hundred lashes and stoning.' That sentence is directly attributed to the Prophet, blessings and peace of Allah be upon him, and narrated in his *Saheeh* thirty-one-ninety-nine."

Reza, her face red, glares at the Imam.

"With all due respect, Imam Jaloliddin, this woman didn't commit *zina* in Pakistan. She is subject to the laws of this country."

The Imam turns to Reza and flashes a spiteful smile.

"And you no doubt mean to indicate that so are you, which must be the only reason you feel emboldened to speak to an Imam with such insolence. Regardless, as Mr. Burakgazi pointed out, our scholars are debating how to make the punishments for sins more compatible with our modern sensibilities. I get that! Fair enough. However, right now she has two options: she can give precedence to Allah, may He be exalted, and seek that which is with Him of eternal happiness and bliss, or she can continue on this sinful journey.

"So what does that mean in practicality?" he pushes his chair back and stands up. He starts pacing across the narrow space between the table and the wall, clasping his hands together, the fingers interlocking and unlocking. "Here is your husband. He wants to be a father to his son. Let's not forget that the son, too, has been through a lot. He needs his father, who, by all accounts, is a God-fearing, honorable man. But wait!" the Imam pauses, turning to glare at Reza, then Zuleikha, with slick disdain, "not only does he want his son back, he wants *you* back, provided that you promise to never consort with that *Shaitan* again. Do you have any idea how rare that is? Instead of feeling cuckolded like any other man would, should, instead of seeking *Talaq,* which he has perfectly reasonable grounds to seek, he wishes to rebuild the life that you singlehandedly destroyed, all for the sake of his family."

He resumes his pacing, staring at the ceiling as he speaks.

"And what do you have to do to go back to your house? To have your family back the way it was meant to be? To take care of your son, have time to play the piano that your husband bought you as a wedding present? Dare I suggest, someday bear another child again and put all this behind? Do you know what you have to do, my dear?"

The room hangs heavy with silence; the air inside has chilled into knots heavy with derision and foreboding. Zuleikha is aware of life outside the door, of a ball bouncing on the hardwood floor to the syncopated rhythm of some unfamiliar piece of music, like a tribal drumbeat. She feels three pairs of eyes upon her and can only steal furtive glimpses in their directions.

Mr. Burakgazi no longer smiles as he speaks.

"Do you understand what Imam Jaloliddin is referring to, Mrs. Khan? I just want to clarify again the gravity of the charges your husband might be facing. And it seems that he *will* face them in court, because everyone is out to get their pound of flesh. If that happens, there is only one witness whose testimony can acquit him, and that's you. If it is indeed true that your husband did not attack you and cause this miscarriage on purpose, then it is important for you to say so. Once again—we're not representing your husband and this is not something he told us to tell you, remember—but your speaking up will save everyone, not least of all your son, a lot of hassle now, won't it?"

"I'm sorry, but in all sincerity I think I'd like to give this young woman a chance to think things through," Reza says. "And as grateful as I am to your organization for supporting mine, I have to say that I have been biting my lips so much for the past thirty minutes that they're about to start bleeding. All this is too much for Zuleikha—for *anyone*—to absorb. She is still taking pain medication, for crying out loud!"

"If you say so, Dr. Yousef, and I trust that you'll give her all the good counsel she needs," Imam Jaloliddin replies, finally sitting back down. "But you will forgive me for telling her one more thing?"

From beyond his eyeglasses, the Imam's brilliant eyes twinkle with malice as they continue to rest upon Zuleikha with a singular determination. Despite cold air now blowing in at full blast, his forehead remains stippled with sweat.

"It may seem like progress to you that we live in a society where every effort is made to accept, endorse even, every form of deviance, and every roadblock put up in front of those that value and wish to practice simple, traditional family lives. But I'd like to remind you that Allah has never cared whether a sin was committed in the Year of the Elephant or the Year of Farewell or now or a hundred years from now, nor does he care if it is committed here in the United States or your homeland of Pakistan or Mr. Burakgazi's homeland of Turkey or my homeland of Uzbekistan or wherever Dr. Yousef's homeland happens to be. Remember, soon this life ends and we die and our bodies disintegrate. If you knew your Quran, if you were more familiar with the *al-Furqaan,* you would know that when you await reckoning and recompense, the same *Shaitan* who led you astray from the Quran is ever a deserter in your hour of need. It will be too late then to bite your hand and cry, 'Ah! Woe to me! Woe to me!'"

***

On their way back, Reza and Zuleikha get stuck in afternoon traffic on the LBJ.

"I know you are sitting right next to me in this car, but where are you, really?"

"There was an email the other day," replies Zuleikha, "about a summer piano training program in New Mexico. I was just thinking how wonderful it would be to get away from the heat of Texas summer."

"I'm sure that would be lovely, both practically and metaphorically. And I'm glad that you're not stewing over what the Imam said."

Ahead of them, four lanes of traffic squeeze into two as cars and trucks snake their way through a construction zone. Dump-trucks, front-end loaders, bulldozers, cranes and excavators dot the shut-down lanes, and massive mounds of dirt rise up in hill formations on either side of the freeway.

"The reason I was thinking about the program is because I'm trying *not* to think about what the Imam said, Reza."

"I know, but it's his job to be dramatic, to try to put the fear of God into you. And he put on a good show, I have to admit. But I've been meaning to ask you something: what happened, Zuleikha?"

"I know you're not married, but have you ever been in love?"

A look of determined chasteness settles on Reza's face. "I'm sorry, dear, but if I am to help you in any way, we can't let our conversations be about me. Nothing personal, just lessons learned from past experience."

Zuleikha leans her head against the passenger-side window and apprehends the chaotic scene outside with an odd, confused sense of resignation, but she does not say anything. Groups of construction workers wearing hard-hats move earth and rocks, level the roadbed, dig trenches for drainage ditches. They install cones, signs and barricades; act as flagmen and stop and direct traffic; use jackhammers to break up existing pavement; use asphalt heaters and cement mixers and pour in new concrete. The muted hum and rattle of their work seep into the car, as do occasional whiffs of burning oil and tar.

"Okay," says Reza, "there are a few other things I've been meaning to talk to you about. One—I can't tell you how proud I am of Wasim, and of how well he is adjusting to his new surroundings. He's shy, I know, but behind that façade is a real charmer. I know you must be proud. If he keeps asking about his father, let him continue to see the counselor. Sonia is very good with this kind of thing.

"Two: I am not going to tell you what to do, but I'll tell you that you have to put your mind to work and decide what to tell the domestic violence investigator. Because they want to speak to you yesterday. Tomorrow we're going to get your stuff, but after that, you *have* to meet with them. You are their star witness."

"I need a little time to recover from today," Zuleikha says.

"I'll see what I can do. There's one other thing I wanted to mention: you know I keep a close eye on what goes on at the shelter, and it hasn't escaped my attention that the other girls haven't warmed up to you yet. All I can tell you is to keep trying. It'll happen."

With a rueful smile, Zuleikha responds, "Well at least you didn't remind me about the feast again. I'm afraid my cooking will never make me any new friends, Reza. But you were asking me earlier what happened. You really want to know? What happened was that my Papajaan knew someone who had a connection with the customs department in Pakistan. He built up a collection of confiscated contraband books and movies and albums to rent out the back door, without ever understanding what any of them were all about. He was trying to save for my dowry, so that I could live the life he couldn't. And he let me read those books, watch those movies, listen to those songs, so that I could become familiar with the life that awaited me."

"And that worked?"

"From them I learned—thought I did—how to fall in love, when really all I did was fall in love with the idea of falling in love. Then he found me a man he thought was perfect, paid his dowry, married me off and sent me over here. And I did fall in love, except I fell in love with someone else. That's what happened. That's my story. According to Imam Jaloliddin, what happened is that the *Shaitan* led me astray from the Quran, and now it is time to give precedence to Allah."

Reza reaches across the seat and takes Zuleikha's hand. She keeps it there and they crawl along with traffic a little longer until the receding sunlight hits them square in the eyes, and both have to reach forward to pull down the sun visors.

"They are going to call these managed lanes as opposed to regular toll roads," Reza says to the windshield. "Instead of fixed rates, the toll will adjust depending on the speed of traffic and the number of drivers who want to use the managed lanes. So during rush hour, you'll have to pay more. I heard on the news it's the first one of its kind in the whole country. The goal is to maintain an optimal speed of fifty miles per hour."

"So, we'll all arrive at our extinction at an optimal speed—just as God intended."

Laughing, Reza says, "I'm not ashamed to admit that I find that amusing. It's almost poetic, that observation, and it gives me no small measure of pleasure. It also tells me something; tells me that you're not into God as much as a certain Imam, for example. But are you into poetry, dear?"

"No. Novels, yes, but there was no market for poetry as far as Papajaan was concerned. But I loved it when you recited from the Rubáiyát the other day."

"Thank you. I was just thinking—I mean, I know you miss your piano, but unfortunately that's not something I can do anything about at the shelter. Not for a very long time, unless some rich businessman wants to donate one to us one of these days for his tax write-off. But what I *can* do is loan you some of my books. I think you will find them just as soothing for your soul. In fact, I know just the one I want you to read first. Yes! Kazim Ali. You'll like him."

"Okay," Zuleikha says halfheartedly, settling into a simmer of deep contemplation.

They reach the shelter just as the shadows are lengthening inside the high walls of the compound, stretching across the walkway to the front entrance. Past the reception desk, they find six or seven women huddled outside Reza's office in the grey light of the sliding day. Yusra, visibly agitated, paces the floor, while Huda, the old woman who has gotten into the habit of sitting next to

Zuleikha at the dinner table, occupies the lone chair on the hallway. The others, looking withdrawn, are spread out on the carpet or leaning against the wall.

Their arrival causes a charge of electricity to pass through the coterie. Yusra reaches them with lengthy strides and with an impulsive gesture reaches for Reza's hand, starts howling.

"Where you all afternoon, Reza? Something terrible happen. Atifah, she gone! She left everything. Took only *jihal*. We worry something happen to her."

In a voice that admits of no reply, Reza says, "Okay, so she left. But let's not take one fact and imagine one more and add them up to make it three, Yusra. Let's all go inside my office and we can talk about it, all right?"

She turns the lights on in her office and the others file in behind her.

"I know from moment she come," says Yusra. "She weak, always say she not do anything without him. She think he change. She think she change him, keep family together for *jihal*. I tell her we all feel that way. But she not believe me. She think it really get better. Now she not call all day. Why not call if nothing happen, Reza?"

"I'll follow up with the authorities, and let's all hope she doesn't turn up on the news. But I can almost guarantee that she won't call us until she is ready to leave him again. Why? Because she is embarrassed. She comes here for help, then she goes back. What exactly is she going to call to say: that she's sorry? Let me show you all something."

Reza digs through the shelf behind her desk and the women watch her with an intensity as if the missing woman herself is about to be miraculously pulled out and produced in front of them. The shelves are cluttered with books and papers, cardboard boxes half full of used clothes and toys, containers strewn with office supplies. Out of the heap Reza pulls out a stack of flyers on matted paper, each showing a graphic in black and purple. She hands them out, keeping one for herself and holding it upright on her desk.

"Some of you may already be familiar with this. We call it the Stages-of-Change chart. Starting at the top of these six circles and going clockwise, you've all been through Pre-Contemplation, Contemplation and Preparation; from just being hurt and angry to thinking about it to planning your escape. Now you've taken Action—that's why you're here, right? You've decided to do something about the problem. But what happens next? You can continue with Maintenance, learn to grow and rebuild your lives and your children's, or you can go into this small circle outside the clock, over here: Relapse. Now do you understand where Atifah is?"

"How long you keep her room?"

Reza returns to the chair behind her desk.

"I know you are fond of her, Yusra, and I appreciate it. Here you are, you've learned to fight back and become strong, and now you are protective of someone like Atifah. I'm very proud of that. But you have to understand that there are others here who are ambivalent, who still have doubts. And every once in a while someone will go back to her abuser."

"But you not keep her room?"

The corners of Reza's mouth drop peevishly.

"You know the policy: one week. I wish I could say nobody else needs a room, and keep this one open for as long as...but...if she calls back, when she calls back, we'll do our best to get her back in. Think of it this way: maybe next time she leaves him, she will be a little less scared, and follow through all the steps in the chart without going to Relapse."

Yusra shudders and makes a little utterance of despair. Then she abruptly turns away from Reza and toward Zuleikha, her eyes narrowed and tinged with a naked resentment. "When you go back to he?"

Put in the spotlight in that abrasive manner, a sense of dread seizes Zuleikha and she is unable to find something suitable to say. She demurely affixes her stare straight ahead at the calendar planner on Reza's desk.

"I know everyone's upset," Reza says in a cautionary tone, "but I'd like to remind you all that we're not going to make any progress collectively by saying disagreeable things to each other."

"But is true," Yusra says to Zuleikha. "You do *zina*. Is your fault. Why you not go back to he, make free your room? They say he nice. He good man. He look good too. If you not go back, maybe I go. Take care of him. Or Tanweer. She like him too. Is true, no Tanweer?"

"That's enough, Yusra," Reza says, her voice ablaze. "I'd like to remind everyone again—"

Zuleikha gives a bitter cry and charges at Yusra. But she can't reach her target; someone gets in the way, then someone else pushes her to the side and holds onto her as she flails hysterically. Yusra yells something unintelligible and taunts her, then other voices are raised and a melee breaks out until Reza's loud rapping on the desk with a tape dispenser captures everyone's attention.

"Stop it. Now!" barks Reza.

A small measure of calm is finally restored in the room. Faced with a wall of leery grimaces, and unable to bear the misery of the day any longer, Zuleikha finally extricates herself from the woman who's been holding her, and runs out of Reza's office in a furious gallop.

She stands by a very large office window at one of the higher floors of the Courts Building on Riverfront Boulevard, staring at the broad, muscular torso of the city proudly stretched out in front. The downtown high-rise buildings to the east, all the way to the Reunion Tower with its caged globe, gleam in the brilliant sunlight, a panoply of chrome and silver and glass and steel. They seem to her the flexing muscles of a fearless being, toned and cut from strenuous workouts requiring a rigor, determination and discipline alien to her; and somewhere, hiding behind those muscles, she senses, beats the heart of the city, while the vivacious traffic that flows through the intricate network of veins and arteries—the ramps and interstates and city streets—pump into that heart the blood that gives it surreal life.

There is a short, urgent knock on the door before it's opened. A woman's head peeks in at first, catches Zuleikha's eyes and meets them with a dazzling smile, before the rest of her person enters the room, carrying a shopping bag that she places on the floor. "Zuleikha," the woman says with a cool sense of familiarity, as if she has known that name since childhood and grew up playing with a girlfriend by the same name, as if Zuleikha is no different to her from Linda or Sally.

The woman extends her hand, and in her heels she is almost as tall as Patrick, but it is her astonishing beauty, punctuated by her ocean-blue eyes, that makes Zuleikha catch her breath at her throat. The woman takes Zuleikha's hand and shakes it, then a look of enormous compassion descends upon her face and she murmurs, "Oh, come on," and with an impulsive gesture pulls Zuleikha into a hug.

Zuleikha feels like a klutz when released from the hug, next to this remarkable woman in the navy striped pantsuit with the peace brooch pinned to the lapel. Her silk shirt is as aquamarine as her eyes, her golden blond hair lightly marcelled in the style of Zuleikha's favorite starlets from a bygone era—Monroe and Gardner and Hayworth— and parted to the right, not a strand out of place.

"Zuleikha, it is so nice to finally meet you."

"That's very kind of you. I'm sorry, Ms.?" Zuleikha murmurs.

"No, no! We're very informal here. So, just Jane, plain Jane, your District Attorney," the woman says with a short laugh. "Unlike your name, which is so beautiful! If you don't mind, what does it mean?"

"It's just a name. But thank you."

"The ADA who's handling your case will be here in just a moment—you'll like him—as well as an investigator, who has to be present. Don't worry; it's standard protocol. But I just wanted to pop in first and meet you in person and tell you how much I admire your courage."

Jane continues to press her hand to the small of Zuleikha's back, as the two now stand side by side, looking outside. Zuleikha feels surprised at the amicability of this woman she would have expected to be more professional and distant.

"From up here, it looks so daunting out there; doesn't

it? Like a wild beast, and here we are in its belly."

"I was just thinking something similar," Zuleikha says.

"We must be kindred souls, or what do they say?—soul sisters or something! Have you heard about the Trinity River Corridor Project?"

"I'm not sure."

"These are exciting times for the metroplex, Zuleikha. The plan is to change the shape of the entire downtown, to breathe even more life into it, by changing our relationship with this incredible asset, this river, running right through its heart. Oh yeah, they have YouTube videos and everything. People are finally recognizing that this place can become one of the truly great, cosmopolitan areas of the entire country—no, the world, so that bright young people like you will want to come here. That is why I was so excited to run for office. Come on, let's sit down and talk for a minute. Do you want something to drink by the way? Coffee? Tea? Soda?"

In that large corner office, they sit on the couch a few feet from the window. Jane's unexpected kindness touches Zuleikha she knows not why, and she feels a little taken aback that the powerful woman now sitting next to her should be so demonstrative.

"Tea. Thank you."

"Don't mention it, tea it is," Jane says.

She excuses herself and walks to the desk at the far corner, speaks on the phone. Returning to her seat, she reaches into the bag and pulls out a gift basket, hands it to Zuleikha. The basket contains cookies and wafer snacks and a ceramic mug with floral patterns.

Zuleikha turns away from Jane.

"I don't know if I can accept this," she says. "In my

custom, in my family's custom, I am supposed to give you something back."

"Oh stop. It's just something from one woman to another that she considers a hero, that's all. You are a hero to me, to this community, to all of us. And I also have something for your son. Hope he likes it."

Jane pulls out a teddy bear and places it next to Zuleikha just as a young woman enters the office with a tray, followed by two men, both young—not much older than her, in their thirties at most—and both wearing suits cut fashionably close to the skin. The men pull up upholstered chairs and take seats on either side of the couch where the two women sit.

"How about I put all these back in the bag, Zuleikha. Let me introduce you to Scott. He's one of our Assistant District Attorneys, and he'll walk us through. And Travis here is an investigator with my office. Now I know you've already met with a DV investigator, but Travis's job is to make sure that if any new evidence emerges during this discussion, he records it and passes it on to the defendant's attorney."

No more chaff is bandied about the room. Jane takes a sip of tea and clears her throat. Her solemn demeanor indicates she is ready to get on with the business of upholding the law of the land.

"We have all read the reports, Zuleikha, and I think I understand where you're coming from. But now that you have had a chance to rest and clear your head, let's go through it all one more time, okay?"

"I do not know what's in the reports. And my own memory is very sketchy."

"Of course, Mrs. Khan—Zuleikha," Scott says, his large

brown eyes full of warmth. "Why don't we go down the reports in order, beginning with what the police had to say? The Irving first responders noticed abrasions under the chin, swelling in your neck, face, and eye. Your voice was raspy, you were panting and had trouble speaking and swallowing when they arrived at your home. There was involuntary urination, not to mention—"

Zuleikha looks down to find her teacup shaking in her hand, and puts it down on the table in front of the couch. She realizes she has lost track of the train of Scott's words and gives him a passing glance. She finds it unfathomable that a person can continue to speak in so sensible a tone while uttering such cruel, vulgar things.

"I'm sorry, Zuleikha, but we have to do this, so we might as well get it over with, okay? It's vitally important that you know and understand what happened and agree with the facts, so that when you are on the witness stand, there are no surprises. We'll prepare you for testimony and their cross, of course, but right now let's focus on getting your story straight. Now, let's talk about the EMT folks. They reported *petechiae* on the neck and face and ruptured capillaries in the white portions of both eyes, all signs of suffocation and manual strangulation."

"The domestic violence investigator tried to explain these things when we met on Tuesday, but to be honest I still do not understand what half of that means," Zuleikha says.

Jane puts down her own cup of tea, takes the hand that is hanging by Zuleikha's side and presses it.

Scott continues, "What that really means is assault family violence by choking. And in the state of Texas, that's a felony. That is before we get to the ER surgeon's report:

placenta abruption due to blunt force trauma on the fetus, resulting in miscarriage, which required an extremely risky D and E procedure—that's Dilation and Evacuation—to clean the uterus to prevent infections. That's what they had to do to save your life."

Zuleikha snatches her hand away from Jane, putting it up to her breast. She is suddenly aware of how chilly the room is, and wishes she was wearing—if not a jacket like Jane—at least a sweater. Jane does not flinch; she merely clasps her hands together on her lap before speaking.

"I know it's hard, Zuleikha," she says. "We see this every day. It's a miracle you survived. I would go so far as to call it destiny, and I have no doubt that God—no matter which God you believe in—has great plans in store for you. But we have to go back to the miscarriage for a second; okay, Zuleikha? Travis, can you please explain?"

The athletic, buzz-cut wearing Travis, who has remained silent until now, coughs like a cold engine sputtering into life, and opens the binder he's been holding in his hands. The siren of a police car gets louder as it approaches the building. Travis waits until it recedes before reading from his notepad.

"The medical report is clear: the fetus was viable and perfectly normal. She's already given birth to one healthy boy, had no prior miscarriage, and there was no indication in any of the regular exams of any risk with this pregnancy." Now he looks up and addresses her directly. "We've reviewed them all, Zuleikha. The point being that the miscarriage could have only been caused by what your husband did."

The start Zuleikha gives shakes her entire body, and she pushes her feet to the ground as though to spring up.

"That's feticide, Zuleikha," Jane jumps in, "and the laws of our state allow the killing of a fetus to be prosecuted as murder regardless of the stage of development, except when the woman is seeking an abortion voluntarily. Which is a whole different can of worms that we won't get into, but clearly, you were not looking for an abortion that night. So it might please you to know that we can rely on legal precedent in this case. In fact, there's case law going all the way up to the Court of Criminal Appeals. And I am here to promise you that we'll get him for that."

"You'll get him? How is that supposed to please me, Jane? First of all, I don't think Iskander was choking me. We were pushing each other, and he tried to slap me, I think, then I fell. The rest is a blur, but I don't think he tried to choke me."

Jane closes her eyes, lets out a long sigh, and rubs her temples. "Zuleikha, will you please excuse us for a moment? You don't have to leave, just give us a second."

The District Attorney gets up, and the two men follow suit. They walk to her desk and huddle around. Jane searches through a stack of binders until she finds one she's looking for. Pointing to whatever is inside it, she whispers animatedly.

She looks out the window into a rhombus of clear, barren blue sky. For the first time she notices the ripple-folded, rich navy curtains hanging on either side of the wide window. What kind of District Attorney hangs satin window curtains in her office? She steals a glance at the District Attorney that does that and finds her engrossed in a deep conversation with the two members of her staff, poring over pictures on her desk. She looks back out the windows. The curtains, held in place with tiebacks, remind her of the recurring dream she used to have. In it, she is already seated at the piano, centerstage, surrounded by the orchestra, all at the ready.

Now the curtains are pulled back and held in place, and a hush settles in.

With every taut fiber of her being, she resists looking up to make eye contact with Papajaan. Her family—her guests of honor—is seated in a private box. They wear new clothes purchased just for the occasion. Papajaan has trimmed and oiled his mustache. Mamajaan has borrowed earrings from her sister, a brocade gold necklace from their next-door neighbor's wife. That woman has never cared for Zuleikha practicing on her Casio every morning and evening, and she has let it be known that she sees no utility in that exercise, only mere fancy on the part of Papajaan; but otherwise she is an agreeable woman who hasn't minded loaning Mamajaan one of her many necklaces for a very special evening.

But what is she, Zuleikha, wearing? That depends on the day of the dream. It's usually gold and yellow, something made of a very rich, delicate fabric, but of not too intricate a pattern. Or gold and black. Tonight, it's gold and ivory.

Now the audience rises and politely applauds. Again she resists the temptation to look for her family. The conductor is prim. He smiles warmly, politely takes the concertmaster's hand for a brief moment, nods graciously at the soloist. The soloist nods back before turning her attention back to the fabulous instrument at her charge. The soloist is ready to publicly embrace Edvard Hagerup Grieg and boldly proclaim her love for him. "Look,

Papajaan," she wants to tell her father. "No need to find a foreign husband. I can take it from here. This was worth it, after all."

The introduction to the concerto begins with its stupendous flourish, but then someone in the audience starts laughing. Indeed, someone is laughing; that's the loud, lecherous, laughter of a lunatic. People shush. Someone barks at the imposter to pipe down, but where is this person? The imposter can't be found, while the laughter not only lingers, it gets louder. The orchestra pauses. She does too. Other members of the audience begin to whistle. She realizes that they all look like Grieg. She used to find it startling how much her favorite composer resembled Einstein, but now she knows who that is. The auditorium is full of Griegs, and they are all whistling at her, the soloist.

This was not the dream she ever had. Jarred to her core, Zuleikha rises to leave, but a small crown of vertigo spins inside her head. She sits back down and calls out to Jane. "Are we almost done?"

Jane and the men pause their intent conversation and look up. The District Attorney says to them in a low voice, "No, we'll do this now." She stands up and walks back to the couch, sits down. The men follow and take their seats.

"Zuleikha, I can't discuss the specifics of any other case by name with you, understand?" Jane says. There is a sudden rigidity in her eyes. "But let's say, hypothetically, that there is another young woman in Irving. She's very pretty, just like you, and very well-dressed and stylish, maybe a little younger, around twenty-five. But her English is not like yours. She's a terrified young mother in a foreign land. She's fed up though—with her husband—

and one day she finds out about this new shelter that just opened for Muslim women and she runs away from home with her kids. The shelter calls police like they are supposed to, the police send an investigator, who gives us a call, and one of my attorneys speaks to her, tells her what the options are. And basically, there are no options; there is no report of domestic disturbance, no 9-1-1 call— apparently she doesn't even know how to call the police! Her husband has been telling her that if she squeals, he will divorce her and she will lose her immigration status. Now I know that *you* already have your green card and therefore immigration is not a factor in your situation, but just in case you've ever wondered the same thing or felt similarly threatened, you should know that in this country, we have protections in place for vulnerable women in your...this position. So anyway, back to our hypothetical friend. See, she doesn't know any of this! There's no evidence, therefore no case. She panics, goes back to her abusive husband."

Jane's manner of speaking suggests that while it is perhaps not appropriate for her to be having this discussion with Zuleikha, the fact that she has given Zuleikha a present at least partly compensates for it. Zuleikha feels vexed by this, not to mention a touch of impatience, about being compared to someone who—as Yusra had already pointed out to her so bluntly—bears no such connection to her.

"We never talked. I'd barely been at the shelter before she was gone."

Jane steals a glance at Scott, makes the faintest flicker of a wink at him.

"We're talking in hypothetical, remember? But here's

the thing, hypothetically: she wears these beautiful face covers, right? The other women at her mosque are jealous she has so many of them; they have these Arabic inscriptions, they are made of very high-quality silk, etc., etc. But what nobody knows is that the reason she's been wearing them may not be just to make a fashion statement, but to hide choke marks on her neck. Yes! Apparently her husband has even put a dog-collar on her, kept her tied to a leash. Not once, many times. So the question—and you don't have to be familiar with the Power and Control Wheel to know the answer—the question is this: do you think those choke marks will go away on their own, or do you think she'll get new ones now that she's gone back to him?"

"Jane, unlike Atifah's—that woman's—husband, Iskander never hurt me. He smirked and treated me like a child sometimes, made fun of me, which made me feel foolish and angry. He lost his temper once on the freeway—not at me, but at another driver. He has a thing about aggressive drivers; he was in a motorcycle accident once. But he never hurt me."

"So we are told. We are told by his lawyer that there will be witnesses who testify what a model citizen he is, that he wants you—his family—back. But do you really expect a man who's facing felony charges to say anything else? Do you expect his lawyer to coach him to say anything else? And when you say that he never hurt you, you forget that he did, in fact, hurt you, when he got mad. That's what matters, and that is where the experts come in, Zuleikha. I should tell you, by the way, that I have a degree in psychology, yeah, double major,"—Jane laughs and rolls her eyes—"but for these types of situations we bring in folks with real in-depth expertise. There'll be a renowned professor talking about all this research: something called psychometric typology of domestic violence offenders. Yes, that is a thing and there is even a scientific publication for it called—what is it called, Scott?"

"*The Journal of Interpersonal Violence*," Scott responds. "Zuleikha, this gentleman is going to talk about the findings of a research paper from Cambridge University on intimate partner violence, and he will walk the jury through all this homicide data, and discuss these scientific models called ABCX and DLM and talk about what some famous scientist named Finkelhor had to say about all this, but basically what it all boils down to is this: Iskander Khan belongs to a group of people known as low pathology perpetrators. The research shows they have generally normal personalities and are rarely violent, but in certain situations, when the time is right—or wrong, when you are on the receiving end of it—especially in their intimate relationships, they are just that. Violent."

The thrust of what Scott says and Jane says and Travis says, so little of which she can follow except for their singular direction, wears Zuleikha down. She wonders if she looks as fatigued as she feels.

Jane seems to sense Zuleikha's fatigue too, only now, she no longer expresses concern or sympathy as a friend might.

"Let me tell you about an incident that happened a few years ago. South Dallas. Guy gets girl pregnant, starts seeing someone else. She calls the new girlfriend and tells her she is carrying his child. New girlfriend confronts him, he tells her he will take care of old girlfriend. What does he do? Pumps a 20-gauge shotgun into her, killing her and her unborn baby. Different circumstances, I know, but very similar situation from a legal perspective: capital murder, which is *this* close to what could have happened in your case. Now this man, Lawrence, appealed—well, his lawyers did—and the Court of Criminal Appeals upheld his convictions. The end result? Life in prison. Now obviously, Mr. Khan is looking at neither the same charges nor the same sentence, because he didn't also kill you on top of killing your unborn child, but do I take a chance that he gets away this time and then finishes you off at the next opportunity? Then what do I tell your son? What do I tell the people of this county who voted me into office, after I promised in my campaign that I was going to stop this revolving door for criminals—that's what the incumbent, my predecessor, used to do, Zuleikha: offer serious criminals plea bargains—but you tell me, what do you think am I supposed to do here?"

Zuleikha tries to imagine having to take Wasim to prison to visit his father, but the very thought of it mortifies her and makes her pale. She finds it incomprehensible that Iskander, for all of his lack of warmth, should find himself in such a cold environment as prison for something that happened in the blink of an eye, whether she can ever forgive him or not. She looks at Jane and sees the prosecutor's face grave in repose, but cannot tell what Jane is thinking.

"Jane, Jane, you've got to believe me! Believe me, I do not love my husband, which is why I did what I did—*you* know what I did! But he does not deserve this. He's a good father, and our son does not deserve to lose his father like this!"

Jane reaches across and pats Zuleikha's hand, her

deliberate and distinguished voice now quite low.

"This can only be a cultural thing. I think the reason you're saying that is because that's how you were brought up. Or is it that the woman who runs that shelter told you to say these things? Let me ask you something, Zuleikha, and I want you to look me in the eye and give me a straight answer: did anyone train you to plead with me on Iskander Khan's behalf?"

"No! I am speaking for myself; please, Jane. Iskander does not belong in a jail."

Feeling incredibly weary, Zuleikha looks down and realizes that again she has withdrawn her hand from Jane's and is now gripping her fist so tightly that her knuckles shine.

Jane takes off her smile as if it is no more than an accessory. She concocts meaningful stares in the directions of her two subordinates, but Zuleikha is unable to fathom what meaning they carry. Her jaw is set in a rigid square and her eyes are cold enough to be molten water surrounded by polar icecaps.

"Are you saying that you do not want to testify in court?"

Zuleikha covers her face in her hands.

"I hate to say this to you Zuleikha, but just in case," Jane continues, "just in case someone who is *not* a lawyer has filled your head with some crazy idea that you can claim spousal or testimonial privilege or something like that, let me remind you that in this case it's a moot point. There *is* such a thing called testimonial privilege, yes, but it does not extend to a proceeding in which one party is accused of a crime against his or her spouse. In other words, I have the ability to subpoena you. And if you still do not show up in court, the state will get a writ of attachment and send a Sheriff's Deputy to go out and find and drag you to court. There's already debate in my department to release the press hounds and publicly shame you—I can get a reporter from the Morning News over here before you can reach the downstairs lobby—but I really don't want to make life any more difficult for you and your son. At the same time, though, you have to cooperate here too."

"No, no!" Zuleikha wails.

"No, as in you don't understand, or no, you do and don't want to go through all this trouble for nothing? Listen, Zuleikha, I hate to be harsh, but I won't be doing my job if we were not having this discussion right now. And I'm telling you this as a former prosecutor who's tried all kinds of capital cases and felonies: with or without your cooperation, we *will* get this conviction. We don't need your testimony with the grand jury, and we don't need it for the trial, because Scott can easily convince a jury that you have been manipulated and are scared, and that this is—like I said—an ingrained cultural fear in you. The evidence, the testimony from the cops and the medical professionals, is *that* overwhelming."

Emptied of tears, Zuleikha gets a tissue out of her purse and blows her nose, gets another and wipes her eyes. She stands up and walks over to the window, looking out into the urban maze outside, feeling as heavy as the concrete that holds up the mighty overpasses.

Jane walks over and stands by her side.

"Zuleikha, a few weeks ago I got a tour of the SPCA. They walked me past all these dogs in their cages. There was this one lab-mix—oh, you should have seen her—I had them bring her out and we played for a few minutes. She had different colored eyes, and she loved to give kisses. I almost took her home. Would have, if I didn't already have a dog. Another rescue. I just can't imagine why someone would want to hurt these things, you know? It's frustrating as hell—our animal cruelty unit has one prosecutor and one investigator right now—and all I can do is add another prosecutor, *maybe*, if there's a little wiggle room in the budget next year. But you know what's really frustrating, Zuleikha? That these beautiful souls cannot talk in our language and tell us what their horrible owners did to them. Do you know what I'm getting at?"

Zuleikha wipes her eyes again and forces a ghastly smile.

"I can see why they elected you, Jane. You're very good."

"I don't think you mean that as a compliment, Zuleikha, but it doesn't matter," Jane says. "It's okay if you question my agenda—I do have one, and I'm not going to deny it. My agenda is to protect you, and every other person who lives in this county, by making sure that justice is served. But you're smart enough to know that the people who want you to keep your mouth shut have their own agenda too, aren't you? It could be argued that even your advocate at the shelter has her own agenda, fueled by her own Mother Teresa complex. She needs victims like you to save, make her living. The more of you, the more job security for her, and the more like a martyr she gets to feel. Ultimately, it becomes a matter of whose agenda aligns with yours. And after you've had some time to think about it, the answer will become pretty clear. Go back to your shelter and think about it, Zuleikha. But in the meantime, we'll move forward, and Scott will meet with the defense attorney for the announcement settings like he's supposed to every three weeks. But he's not offering an easy-*peasy* plea deal on this one, just so you know. Nor is he going to agree to visitation—which they say they're going to petition the judge for—without the proper precautions. That means the defendant has to go through all the steps: batterer's intervention program, parenting classes, the whole bit. Then he can see his son—and only starting with supervised visitation at first. We're going to fight this all the way."

Zuleikha turns around to look first at Scott, then Travis.

"And you two are both very good. You have to be, to be working for her."

Neither man responds. They continue to sit, unperturbed, holding her in their expressionless gazes. The thought crosses Zuleikha's mind that the two men, professionals, are well versed in the art of handling provocation with patience and shrewdness. But it also seems to her, as she watches them, fascinated, that an otherworldly, invisible apparatus has exsanguinated them, converting both into statues.

"You're telling me that the District Attorney met you in person and told you all this?" Reza asks later with widened eyes, after Zuleikha has given her an account of the meeting, leaving out only the part about Jane questioning Reza's motives.

Zuleikha feels uncomfortable with Reza's mischievous smile. Jane's remark about the agenda of victims' advocates, which had seemed crude and crass at the time, creeps up in Zuleikha's mind again, making her wonder if Reza does, indeed, have some ulterior motive lurking beneath her ebullient patina of neutrality.

"Well, we didn't discuss the Dallas Symphony's concert calendar, Reza. She's the District Attorney. Isn't that her job?"

Reza smiles mischievously and taps her ballpoint pen on the desk. "Zuleikha, the DA's job is to go to meetings and functions. She gets reports and gives press conferences. She's an elected official and the face of the department; she does not get her hands dirty with individual cases, the attorneys that work under her do that. Bet I know why she's so interested in yours, though."

"Reza, I'm exhausted and hungry and haven't seen Wasim all day. I just cannot handle any more intrigue today."

"I'm sorry, dear, but this is something I'm not going to explain; you should do this on your own. Go online and look up our District Attorney sometime, see what she's been up to since taking office—actually, since even before that. Then you'll figure it out."

In the days that follow, while Wasim spends the mornings with the other children in the daycare, Zuleikha, driven to misery from missing her piano, spends her time catching up on news articles and editorials about the twin controversies unfolding in the metroplex like the pitchers of the carnivorous monkey cup plants that trap living things alive in their trunks: the goings-on at the office of the Dallas County District Attorney who has only been in the office for a few months, and the furor—spreading beyond the confines of the state now, but with Irving at its epicenter—over the now operational north Texas Islamic

Tribunal. While the domestic violence case involving the Khans of Irving no longer commands the headlines, it runs through both stories like the modal rhythmic cycles of a quintuple meter in ancient Abbasid songs.

Zuleikha discovers that the same cool, professional Jane who so emphatically lectured her about the perils of harboring shameful secrets tried to not only conceal one of her own, but also actually lied about it, claiming that she was merely recovering from back surgery when in truth she had checked into a rehab center for prescription drug addiction. Zuleikha reads about the din surrounding Jane's firing of her long-time friend as her second-in-command, and about candidates already vowing to challenge her in the next election. Is it any surprise then—Zuleikha can't shake off the question—that a District Attorney embroiled in controversies would seize upon the opportunity to try a Muslim man for fetal homicide?

Then there is the Irving mayor, a woman she has never met and would have been hard pressed to even name or point out in a picture just three weeks ago, who mentions Zuleikha by name and writes of her situation—in a newspaper op-ed—as precisely the type of case that should not be arbitrated at the tribunal she opposes. Zuleikha can't help but be suspicious of a deft complicity between the ambitious mayor and the beleaguered district attorney.

She feels incredible about playing small but crucial roles in both strange and unreal stories, like the mother in the final scene of *My Landlady*—one of her favorite movies, when the audience knows little about the real Zuleikha that has lived and breathed for twenty-nine years before her cameo. That was not politics; that was real.

Sleepless nights bleed into bleary days. After the first week, Wasim stops asking about his father. Zuleikha feels no sudden stream of tears gushing up inside. The sky, however, does the crying for her. When she goes for walks on the Campion Trail during lulls in the rain—sometimes with Wasim and sometimes by herself—she finds the low-lying parts of the maze of pathways and surrounding fields waterlogged, impossible to traverse. The sights appear to her as unfamiliar paintings of a familiar landscape, the effect of an avant-garde painter's violent chiaroscuro, and they serve as a confusing background to the desultory strife inside her.

Curiously, while Imam Jaloliddin's astronomical arrogance and unctuous browbeating had only furthered her distance from her marriage, Jane's supportive and carefully choreographed act (she has come to decide that's what it was: a practiced put-on by a polished professional) managed to accomplish quite the opposite. Sitting in that tastefully decorated, air-conditioned office, she had felt not just a rush of relief that neither she nor Wasim had ever been subjected to such cruelties as some other women, but also an unexpected little thrill of pride to be able to claim that her marriage has not been as bad as those of others, and that Iskander was not such a beast as some other men. That last bit of realization about someone that she was never able to truly love, when given the chance, was what had made her feel so tortuously guilty, and caused her to speak up in his defense.

Now it seems to her—while she flips through Kazim Ali's poems or combs Wasim's hair—that everything is a truth laced with untrue motivation, or a lie coated with veracious sincerity, and they all try to explain a lot about something to someone, though not especially to the one most responsible, most affected, and perhaps most crucial to what happens next: her.

One sultry evening, the women and the children are all gathered in the dining room. The air in the corner where the little ones sit is full of the alacrity and rambunctiousness that is peculiar to childhood. At their table, Huda keeps insisting—in her mixture of amorphous Arabic that Zuleikha doesn't grasp and unsubtle gestures that any human with a semi-functional brain can make sense of—that her companion is turning into an unsightly stick and should therefore eat more. Zuleikha, feeling particularly lethargic, admits to herself that perhaps Huda does have a point. She takes a few more bites, but the food on the plate—although not of her own making—tastes as if it is.

Across the room, the children sound as children should, until they suddenly don't. The shriek of a young voice rises from the corner and pierces the room. Then just as precipitously a hush settles upon it, but only momentarily, before a clamor breaks out. Zuleikha looks up from her plate just in time to see Yusra marching purposefully toward the children's table, trembling with menace. Reaching the table, she yanks her son—a boy of no more than eight, as voluble and overweight and prone to wild gesticulations as she is—out of his seat and starts pummeling him. Another woman arrives at the two. She tries to intervene by wrestling the boy away at first, and then, failing to do so, wrap her arms around Yusra in an effort to mitigate the fierceness of her punches. But Yusra yields no quarter and continues to assault the boy. And the boy just stands there and takes it. Apart from hunching over and raising his arms to form some sort of protective shield around his head, he does nothing against this grotesque onslaught of blows from his own mother.

Only then, after watching this stunning display of justice being meted out by one mother to her son, does Zuleikha's eyes come to rest on the original victim. To her horror she realizes it is Wasim. Zuleikha bolts from her seat and runs to her child, and only when she gets near him does she realize that his face is smeared with the molten, gold colored cheese, macaroni, and heaps of dark brown, sand-like *cous cous*. His hair, too, is a bleary mess, with streaks of food running through it. Wasim's mouth is agape, but no sound escapes it. Blood drips out of his left nostril. Zuleikha utters a guttural moan and pulls her son close to her chest.

"Water, please! Cold water—I think he broke his nose!"

More women crowd over them. One reaches for the partially empty glasses of water on the children's table and hands them to Zuleikha, who uses them to wash Wasim's face. Her son winces in pain and attempts to pull his face away. A wrinkled hand with veins prominently jutting across it reaches across for the boy's face, and Zuleikha, startled, looks up to see Huda. Her companion bears a look of grim determination as she applies firm pressure, rendering Wasim's face still.

A wad of gauze is thrust forward in her direction. Zuleikha daubs Wasim's bleeding nose with it, and Wasim, his breath constricted, starts whimpering softly.

"Wasim? Wasim, listen to me. I have to take you to see the doctor right now, okay?"

"He punched me, Mamajaan, but I didn't do anything."

"Can you stand up please? Let's go."

"Will I get a shot, Mamajaan?"

"I don't know, Beta, I don't know. Remember that time you felt very hot and we went to that clinic? It's open twenty-four hours and they see you pretty quickly, so we'll go to the same place, okay?"

"I don't remember."

"Beta, they have to see if your nose is broken. If you need stitches." She feels Wasim stiffen in her arms, and adds, "It'll be okay. I'll be right next to you the whole time, all right?"

"Will Papajaan be there?"

Zuleikha replies in a faltering voice, "He can't, Beta. I'm sorry."

"I want to see Papajaan."

Zuleikha picks up her son, but he is not a child anymore; his weight takes her breath away and she feels a little lightheaded. But in other ways he remains a child. He puts his head on her shoulder, the gooey, smelly mess of food on his clothes now smattering against her own. His little curled fist knocks on her shoulder like an antique brass knocker on a heavy teak door. He starts sobbing.

"You get upset if I don't listen to you, but you're not listening to me. I want to see my Papajaan. It wasn't my fault," Wasim says.

Zuleikha is too overcome with emotions to care about whose fault it is and to whom guilt is assigned, for her own sense of guilt overwhelms all others. Letting out an exasperated sigh, she whispers to him, "I'll have to put you down, but if you come with me right now, we'll go to our room so that I can get my purse and the phone, and I'll text Papajaan, let him know what happened—that I'm taking you to the clinic. We'll go from there, okay?"

As they leave the dining room, the last thing Zuleikha sees is Yusra holding her son in a tight embrace, both sobbing.

Inside Examination Room 1 of the clinic, father and mother stand on either side of the chair as the nursing assistant finishes cleaning Wasim's face.

"You're going to feel a little pinch on your nose until these butterflies fly away," the woman says to Wasim, "but tomorrow...do you know what's gonna happen tomorrow?"

Wasim stares suspiciously at her, but he does not speak. A glance passes between his parents, but Zuleikha is unable to read Iskander's face. She is struck once again by how much he seems to have aged in a few weeks: the grays sticking out of his black hair like errant threads in a poorly stitched piece of embroidery. There are heavy, misshapen sacks under his eyes. He looks gaunt; his clothes are loose and his belt is fastened tighter, minuscule cracks showing across the leather around the eyelet that was previously used.

"Tomorrow, you're going to look like a boxing champ."

Wasim smiles—sheepishly—for the first time that evening.

"Your eyes will be black and blue, darker than your nose, even though that's not where you got hurt, right?"

"I'm just glad he didn't break anything," Iskander says, as he has several times already. "Thank you."

"But don't worry, your eyes won't feel any pain," the woman, slim, middle-aged, with blonde and blue highlights in her dark hair, continues with a smile. "In fact, if you do what the doctor said—take this medicine, be a good boy and go straight to bed after you get home tonight—then by the time you wake up tomorrow, you'll barely feel any pain, I promise." She hands him a small plastic cup of clear syrup.

Wasim's hands shake as he swallows the medicine. His eager eyes dart from his father's face to his mother's.

"We'll go home tonight?" he asks Zuleikha.

Zuleikha sucks in her cheeks; her teeth sink into the flesh. "No, Beta," she says, "we'll go back to our place, all right?"

Tears form at the corners of Wasim's eyes. His lips quiver. "But Mamajaan!" he protests.

"May I speak to you outside for a moment?" Iskander asks Zuleikha with a pained, beseeching look in his eyes.

"You're not nice," Wasim continues. "You tell me if I'm not nice, but you're not nice!"

The nursing assistant runs the tip of her tongue over the ring at the edge of her lower lip and steals awkward glances at Zuleikha and Iskander. "I'll be right back with some paperwork to sign, then ya'll are free to leave," she says.

"Mamajaan, you're not nice! I want to go home," Wasim insists.

This accusation, leveled at her by the one person whose birth she considers the single most momentous occasion of her own life, fills Zuleikha with an inexplicable, raw tenderness; she feels like crying. Whatever you do, don't cry, she tells herself.

Iskander says, to the woman this time, "Actually, could you stay here with our son for just a couple of minutes while I speak to her outside?"

Zuleikha feels the ground shifting beneath her feet, and she wonders if yet another earthquake has just struck; there have been quite a few of them in the Irving area recently, most of them merely mild tremors, but some quite violent. From news programs running in the background at the shelter she has become vaguely aware of the debate surrounding whether or not they are caused by some new way of drilling for oil. But nothing else vibrates; the thermometer, the roll of gauze, lay perfectly still on the tray. The rattling sensation persists only within her core. She feels appalled. She starts to say "That won't be necessary" just as the nursing assistant, too, starts speaking.

The woman pauses. Zuleikha pauses too.

"Look, I don't know what the deal is between you two," the woman says sassily, with an emphatic shrug and elaborate hand gestures. "And normally I'd rather sit here and watch your drama than the scripted stuff they put on television and call reality TV, but *right now* you need to work it out and decide what to do about your son. My job is done here—all our jobs are—and it's a good thing you folks are the only ones in here tonight. So I'll wait here with him for a minute, but please!"

Zuleikha knows each of them is watching her, they each seem to be asking: *Well?* She finds herself unable to look Iskander in the eyes; instead, her eyes settle on the small rectangular mirror above the sink. In it, she sees a fraction of her own face, one ear, one earring (her mother's small silver hoop), one eye, open wide. She knows that earring, she recognizes that eye, but it is not the face of the self she knew. She dares not stretch her neck to see the entire face; she dares not shift an inch further right.

"Mamajaan—" Wasim starts again, and Iskander pats his hand, shushes him. "It's all right, Beta. Zu, *please*, can we step outside for a minute and talk about this like adults?"

I have to do this, she tells herself. He is not a violent person, isn't that what I claimed, to the District Attorney, of all people? I believe that to be true. We shared a home; we had a child together. This child, who wants to go back to that home tonight. And this man: he loved me once, he saw me whole, not the fraction that I am now. But I tried to see him whole too, once, even though he, too, turned out to be no more than a fraction of the person I wished him to be. He looks like a scarecrow. He *is* one; I can't be scared of him.

"Zu?" Iskander says.

Zuleikha squeezes Wasim's hand. She bends down to give him a peck. "You wait right here with her, and I'll talk to Papajaan outside. We'll be right back."

Wasim nods, pressing his cheek against the tearstained pillow.

Iskander follows Zuleikha out of the room. As soon as he closes the door behind them, she tells him, "No, Iskander. No! Wasim was hurt, he wanted to see you. So I called you. He's fine now; I have to take him back."

"Zu, he just wants to come home and sleep on his own bed. You can see that, can't you?"

Hearing him call her Zu pricks her like a splinter. "He can't," she whispers hoarsely. "He's not supposed to. And we are not supposed to talk like this! We might be in enough trouble as it is. There are procedures you have to follow in order to have visitation."

"We might be in trouble for trying to do what's best for our child? Do you know how hard it's been to not see him?" he asks, his mouth agape in disbelief, reminding her of Wasim's from earlier in the evening, in the dining hall. Father and son, one so like the other. "There are procedures I have to follow in order to have"—he curls his fingers into quotation marks in the air—"visitation with my own son?"

Flummoxed by the logic of Iskander's words, Zuleikha falls silent.

Iskander leans against the wall, stares out into the dark through the glass windows. "I can't believe this," he whispers. "What happened to you, Zu? We loved each other, didn't we? We were good to each other, and I *know* you were not like this before you met that man. Does the past not matter to you at all?"

"This is hardly the time to have this discussion. What we should do right now is get going, him with me."

"When is the time to have a real discussion? You tell me: when would be a good time for me to say that I still care for you, always have? In court, in front of the world— is that what you want: more public shaming? Would that be a good time to tell you that I miss you both like crazy? That I'm sorry, forgive me?"

"I'm sorry; it's a little late to say those things. We are in a big mess already, please don't make it worse."

"What's the matter with you?" he asks, putting his face in his hands.

"The matter with me is that I'm not going to let you use this situation to manipulate me."

He throws his hands forward in frustration, as if shaking the air. He paces the floor.

"I'm not trying to manipulate you, for God's sake! I'm just trying to tell you that we can put all this behind, go back to being a whole family like we used to be before you—before that man entered our lives. Right now! Instead...do you hear yourself? When did you become so harsh?"

"Maybe you killing our unborn baby, nearly killing me, had something to do with that," she retorts, unable to restrain her anger any longer. "No matter what you say, that much is true. You can't deny that you hit your pregnant wife. It's why I fell. But you know what's funny? Here's your lawyer arguing that you fell on me next, and there's the DA saying there's no way that could have been an accident, but nobody has asked me how I feel about what happened next? Do you want to know?"

"Zu—"

"Don't call me that, please! When I lay there bleeding, with Zafar dying, you never helped me. If you had, maybe we could have saved him. Maybe things would have turned out different, maybe not, but I wouldn't have become so harsh—I don't think I'll ever stop thinking about it. And I thought *I* was dying too, and I had to beg you to help me, get help, and once you left the room to call 9-1-1, you never came back inside."

"I lost that baby too."

His words barely reach her. Weeks of anguish gush out of her, unchecked. "I was in so much pain, if ever there was a need for comfort that was then, but you never—and I can never forgive you for being such a coward. What happened to me, you ask? Well, what happened to you? You used to ride a motorbike! How did you become such a coward? So dispassionate? You can laugh at me for saying this, but all my heroes from all my favorite movies would have helped. Even if I loved you before, I could never, ever, love you after the way you left me then."

"I'm sorry, Zu! I thought I was growing up. Please, let me apologize again—"

"Growing up to become what? You know what? It's pointless. Did you not just hear what I had to say? Because now we really have to go. But let me do what I can to put your mind a little at ease. I'll testify in court that you weren't abusive; I'll testify that you did everything for me and your son, that you were a good father. I'll tell the court that you should be able to see your son, you do deserve it; that I never caught you lying. I'm the one who misled you. Yes. I'll even tell them that I didn't see whether you stomped on me, or as you claim—slipped and fell by accident. Because I didn't really see. But after that it's up to you and your lawyer and the jury and the court. And whoever else is your witness. What happens then doesn't matter to me anymore."

"It matters to me! To Wasim!"

"I agree. But not to me, I want you to understand that. Do you know why?"

The Adam's apple in Iskander's throat bulges, but he doesn't say anything. He stares at her, unblinking, his eyes naked with shock.

"Because whatever happens, whether you're found guilty or innocent, whether you go to jail or not, I want a divorce after this case is done. I want a different life, away from you."

The doorbell chimes. Down the hallway, voices are heard as people enter the clinic.

The nursing assistant opens the door and looks at

Iskander and Zuleikha. "All right, that's enough. We're a one-doctor, one-assistant outfit. There's a new patient I have to intake," she says. "And your son is falling asleep, by the way."

"Yes, we are finished talking. Thank you so much," Zuleikha tells her. Without shutting the door to the examination room behind her, the woman purposefully strides past them toward the front desk. They hear her greet the new arrivals, another woman's bickering voice. The fluorescent light emerging from the room in which Wasim is resting paints a chunky band on the dark hallway carpet, a line of demarcation between Zuleikha and Iskander. "You heard her. Please go inside and say goodbye to Wasim, then I have to take him back."

"Just like that, huh?"

"Yes. Please Iskander, say bye to him. But he has to go with me, and you can see him in the future according to court orders. I'll not be in the way. But for now, can you not make it worse for him?"

"Don't you ever tell me not to make things worse for my son," Iskander says with a savage glare, even though his eyes brim with tears and his voice wavers. He wags his finger as he walks past her and enters the room. "You may have all kinds of other rights by playing victim, but you have no right to do that. Excuse me; I'll just be a moment."

Much later that night, there is a gentle knock on the door as she sits at the desk, reading. Zuleikha's first thought is that it can only be Yusra; she has no inclination to speak to that woman, then or ever again. But then another knock follows. Reza's voice softly calls out, "Zuleikha! Zuleikha, are you still awake?"

Zuleikha cracks open the door.

"How is he?"

"He will be okay. Just a few butterfly stitches, but nothing broken."

"I'm sorry. They called to tell me what happened, but I was out to a play and had my phone turned off, or I would have come earlier."

Zuleikha lets Reza in, who walks over by the bed and stands, watching the sleeping child. Zuleikha sits down again and lets out the sigh she's been holding in all evening. "I made a big mistake tonight, Reza," she mutters.

"Oh no!" Reza whispers. "You called him."

Zuleikha bites her lips and nods. "Now I know why the courts say no contact."

"Did he make a scene in front of Wasim?"

I'm pretty sure we both did, she thinks. "I don't know what to do anymore, Reza."

"I know you're trying, Zuleikha. And I know it's hard."

"Do you? Forgive me, but I'm not sure that you do, Reza. I mean, I know that you understand how hard it is for the other girls. They've been abused, they are innocent, and it's all black and white. But here I am. I only texted Iskander after Wasim became hysterical, Reza. And I wanted to throw a little redeeming light on his nightmare, but then, once Iskander got to the clinic, one thing led to another and it just got ugly—but what else was going to happen? I know I just can't do that ever again, no matter how upset it makes Wasim. But that also makes me feel like I'm the worst person in the world."

Reza sits at the foot of the bed, close to Zuleikha. "You are not, that much I know," she says in a muffled voice.

In the dimly lit room, Zuleikha can't clearly see Reza's face. "Imam Jaloliddin would disagree."

"It does not matter what the Imam thinks," Reza whispers back with urgency. "What matters is what you think."

"Actually, I think what really matters is what the lawyers think."

"Do you want to step outside and talk for a minute? He's not going to stir, not after what he's been through, and not if he's got any children's Tylenol in him, dear," Reza offers. "And if he does, you'll hear him. These walls are paper thin, in case you haven't noticed."

They walk out into the corridor looking out into the parking lot, and past it, acres and acres of neatly lit rows of commercial parking garages leading to the DFW airport.

"You were saying—"

"Reza, even after everything that has happened, even after tonight, I just don't agree with what the prosecutors say: that Iskander is some baby-killer who belongs in jail and doesn't deserve to see his son for a long time."

"Oh, Zuleikha."

"Now do you understand why it's so hard for me?"

A pair of giant trucks rumbles by the freeway beyond the opposite end of the building from where they stand, but they can still feel the reverberations shake the building like a mini earthquake.

"So what is it that you want, Zuleikha?"

"What I want? Ha!" Zuleikha puts withering scorn into the question, and silence falls between them for a while. Leaning against the wall, Zuleikha stares out into the distance past the airport parking garages, where the vast expanse of the airport itself spreads out in the shape of a mini universe with dim lights flickering like faint stars, planets, and moons. Reza stands next to her and gently rubs her lower back.

Finally, Zuleikha breaks the spell of silence. "I'm sorry. I know you do care about what I want. What I want is a clean break so that each of us can start a new life, and by that I do not mean that I want anything to do with the other person. Patrick. What's that Kazim Ali poem?

"'I am no longer that tempest

I will no longer look up and see the absence of trees?'"

"Ah, you've been doing some reading, I see," Reza says. "That makes me so happy, dear.

"'This is not a descent into catacombs, an inevitable combustion,

a darkening into blindness

Rather it is an approach on knees towards true sight.'"

"Thanks again for letting me have the books, Reza. I'd like my future to be something like that. What I mean is that I'd like to live on my own, maybe get away for the summer—I have some money saved away from my piano lessons—like that summer program I was telling you about, then come back and start teaching full time, or maybe apply to a graduate program, I don't know! But what I want more than anything else is for Wasim to have normal relationships with both parents. So that's what I want. But apparently, that's not what the state wants."

"The state may not want what you want, but at least here, you'll get your day in court," Reza chuckles. "Remember, regardless of what happens to Iskander, Wasim can have a relationship with him. Will it be difficult if he's sent to jail? Yes. But impossible? No! But more importantly, what's stopping you from going to that summer program?"

"What's stopping me?" Zuleikha looks at Reza incredulously. "How about all that's happened in the last few weeks? How about the fact that they would have to accept me first? In order to do which, I have to apply. The deadline is in mid-April, I think, so that leaves me what—two weeks?—to call the academy in Pakistan for transcripts, track down instructors for references? No thanks! And can I even leave the area with the court case going on?"

Reza shakes her head and smiles. "Zuleikha, dear, no offense, but that's what I call making excuses. No court will stop a victim—I know, I know, you don't necessarily feel like a victim, but get over it! That's what you are!—and no court will stop a victim from going wherever she wants, as long as she is back when needed at court. That is a point of law; I know, I've been doing this a while, dear. And you won't be needed in court for a long time. Do you know how long it took for that Dallas Cowboy's domestic violence case to come to court? You can go down to my office right now—I'll watch Wasim—and call Pakistan. Just go!"

Zuleikha's heart beats madly and she feels sick with apprehension. There is something so intimate in the feel of the strong press of Reza's hand against her back that she has to bite her lip to prevent herself from crying. But when she looks at Reza, she notices Reza's cheeks glistening in the semi darkness of the dim hallway.

"Zuleikha, look, you said I don't understand your peculiar situation. And maybe you're right. But maybe you're wrong. Do you know what it's like to have to duel with yourself about whether or not to tell the world what your own father has done to you? Do you know what it's like to spend your teenage years feeling guilty about your own body, your own life? About letting any man get close to you?"

"Oh my god! I'm sorry, Reza."

But just as quickly, Reza rubs her cheeks with her open palms and composes herself.

"It's not something one ever gets used to talking about. Nor does it matter anymore. I grew from it, I found the strength to do what had to be done. I found my life's calling out of my experiences, and here you are on the verge of finding yours. You don't belong in this place, and neither does your son. You are the gifted soloist—yes, I know you appreciate that analogy—and here I am the conductor of a floundering orchestra trying to get a ragtag group to take charge of their individual melodies before they can make harmony. Is it any wonder the other women don't like you? They don't like you because they'd give up their kidneys to be in your shoes: you with your driver's license, your car, education, your English, and most of all—ability to make a living. Therefore, as the conductor I have to encourage you to pave your own path. I'll help you with the application: I've forgotten more about writing grant applications than most people will ever learn. You call the district attorney's office tomorrow, let them know your plans. Tell them you'll write to the judge that Iskander should get visitation with his son—you get to do that, you know—then get out of here, will you?"

She stops at a gas station off Interstate-40 west of Amarillo for what she hopes will be the final rest stop before Albuquerque. The westerly sun slinks at a leisurely angle, nearing the end of a good summer day's work of burning the earth brown. While the tank is being filled, Zuleikha and Wasim walk inside the convenience store. They use the restrooms and get a couple of snacks, return to the car. When Zuleikha turns the key in the ignition, the engine springs into life but something feels a little off, in the same manner that a familiar dish one makes every other week tastes a just a little unfamiliar when one has accidentally, for once, forgotten the salt.

Wasim, who has already buckled himself into the booster seat in the back, asks, "What happened to the song, Mamajaan?"

She notices then that the compact disc player has stopped working; in fact, all the lights in the radio panel are out.

"Not sure, Beta. We'll just sing by ourselves the rest of the way, okay?"

"How much longer?"

"About four hours. But if you take a nap, it'll go by quickly, you'll see."

"How long is four hours?"

"That's like from the time I dropped you off at daycare until the end of lunch. But first...first you're going to close your eyes and try to rest, all right?"

A knock on the window puts a stop to their conversation. A young man with mutton chop sideburns and small eyes stands next to the driver's side door. He wears a garage attendant's uniform with the name *Rodney* sewed in red above his shirt pocket. When Zuleikha presses the button, the window does not roll down. The song of freedom that's been singing in her heart comes to a sudden pause, and an unsettling worry descends upon her that she possesses neither the capacity to comprehend the sudden, unknown illness that has befallen her car, nor the time and means to diagnose and treat it.

The man taps her window again. He points to the door handle, motioning her to open it. When she does, he says, "There's cars waiting behind you, lady."

"Sorry! It's just that my radio stopped working, and now my window—"

"For problems you see Anthony, he's the mechanic," the young man whose name could be Rodney says, and he points to the garage that shares a wall with the convenience store. "But you have to move your car away from the pump. You're holding up business here."

She navigates her car through the chaos of other people walking in and out of the convenience store and cars and trucks pulling in and out of the gas station. Reaching the garage, she leaves the engine running and steps out. The air is full of the jaunty rhythms of a country song playing on the radio. Two men working on a jeep that is raised above ground stop their work and watch her walk toward them.

"Anthony?"

The man who steps forward points to the name sewn into his bright blue, grease stained shirt and nods, but he doesn't say anything. He maintains his cool gaze, appraising her with what she senses is more than a passing curiosity. It does not escape Zuleikha's attention when Anthony glances over at her hand to see if she is wearing a ring.

She explains the problem, adding that the electrical short has been there for as long as she has had the car. Anthony continues to nod agreeably, but by now Zuleikha is very aware that Anthony's attention is only half-focused on her words.

When she finishes, he asks, "Are you on television by any chance?"

Caught by surprise, she says, "What? If I was on television, do you think I'd be driving this car? I would hope to fly where we are going."

"True that," Anthony says, flashing a disarming smile. "But then you wouldn't get to experience up close and personal the raw beauty of our countryside. And us folks out here wouldn't get to experience beauties like you passing us by from time to time."

Zuleikha feels befuddled in the face of this sudden, unexpected compliment. Attraction and lust were sensations she had begun to believe she no longer felt. The idea had been forming in her that there was not much left of her for anybody but herself and her son, even anybody's fantasy. But now she can't deny—despite his dirty hands and shirt—a certain attractiveness in this man, Anthony, who appears to be about the same age as her, and who holds his head at an almost arrogant tilt and bears an almost arrogant smile.

"Do you think you can take a look?" she says lamely, a chilly smile on her face.

"Yeah, sure. It could be just the relay, and that's an easy fix. It'll take fifteen, twenty minutes, though. Do you need to visit the store in the meantime?"

"We have what we need," Zuleikha says.

At the mention of *we*, Anthony bends to peer inside the car and notices Wasim in the backseat. "Suit yourself." He points in the distance and adds, "That's the world-famous Cadillac Ranch. You got a camera?"

"What's that?"

"Just some crazy Texas millionaire's idea of fun. If you walk past the pumps, you'll get a decent shot. I wouldn't try to cross the interstate on foot, though, especially with a child."

Zuleikha turns the engine off and hands Anthony the keys, helps Wasim out of the car, and grabs the snacks, the bottles of water, and her purse. As they walk away, the other man calls out, "Real smooth, Anthony," and Anthony replies, "Shut up."

They walk to the edge of the parking lot of the gas station. She rips open the bag of chips and hands it to Wasim, who busies himself with its contents, and proceeds to take a sip of water. Ahead of them is a split highway with traffic flowing in opposite directions, and a pair of frontage roads. Wide medians separate each strip of concrete from the other. Past all that, ten cars rest half-submerged into the ground at an angle. From where they stand, the artifacts themselves appear no larger than individual match sticks lifted up from their book in an unusually symmetrical aspect. Yet the distance lends to them an air strangely spiritual and especially significant. It seems to Zuleikha that by hinging the cars to nature in such an unnatural way, this piece of absurdist art somehow aptly captures the infinite possibilities of this wide-open land and the indomitable spirit of those who occupy it. Vehicles large and small and in all manner of shapes zip by east or west, momentarily blocking their vision like obstacles appearing out of nowhere in a video game. Every once in a while one stops by the roadside attraction and passengers get out, setting out on foot to the collection of automobiles buried in the dirt. A dry breeze blows through the barren landscape, lending the fields the shimmering enchantment of a wild western movie.

Suddenly, Wasim, awhile quiet, tugs at her, hoarsely whispering, "Mamajaan, Mamajaan!"

Zuleikha looks away from the Cadillac Ranch and toward the opposite direction where Wasim is pointing. There, amidst acres and acres of empty farmlands dotted with pumpjacks here and there and rows of wind turbines in the distance, is a steeple. She imagines it belongs to a Baptist or a Methodist church, the houses of worship of those two denominations being the most common ones they have passed for hours on end now. But this one, silhouetted against the sun, is starker and more striking than any she has seen. There are no billboards on the property, no glittery sign asking "JESUS: Do you know him?" Instead, two double-rows of white crosses run north-south and east-west, the latter, running parallel to the highway, and longer than the other; they intersect at the point where the house of worship stands, thereby giving form to a formidable monument in the shape of a cross itself. Zuleikha suddenly feels very uneasy. Everything within her range of vision seems to be the omen of something, but of what she cannot fathom. The crosses bearing east-west lean strangely to the left, as if they wish to take a better peek at her; in the afternoon breeze they appear to shiver a little, or perhaps they are merely shimmying in an optical illusion.

Now several men appear as if out of nowhere from the middle of those fields, and they walk toward the gas station parking lot where they stand. The sight of them in their cowboy outfits, all the way from the hats on their heads down to the boots on their feet, sends a tingle down Zuleikha's spine. Realizing she's sweating, she clasps Wasim's little hand and starts walking. When they reach the small wooden counter of the garage, she notices Anthony and his colleague bent over the open hood of her car, peering in. She emits a little cough, causing both men to look up and turn around.

Anthony steps forward with a friendly smile. "Get any good pictures?"

"I don't have a camera. Did you find out what's wrong?"

"I did," Anthony says quickly, as if he is scandalized by the mere consideration of the possibility that he hasn't. "Unfortunately, it's not the relay like we'd hoped for. I have to open up the back to get to the wiring, figure out exactly where the short is. It's not as easy, it'll take more time, but I can get it fixed."

"How much will that cost?"

"Well, it's mostly just labor. The faulty wire don't cost much to replace, but finding it is the part that takes time. And putting it back together. I'd say you're looking at somewhere between three and four hundred dollars."

Zuleikha winces. "That much!"

"Afraid so. We're talking several hours of work."

"Several hours! I can't wait that long!"

"See, the problem is that it's simply impossible to tell," Anthony says with an apologetic smile and scratching of his chin. "It might take less—time and money both, but I just don't know 'til I open up the thing."

"But that means I'm stuck here tonight! I need to get to Albuquerque before dark, before my son has to go to bed."

"As a certified mechanic I strongly advise—"

"Mamajaan, I'm still thirsty," Wasim says, tugging at her shirt.

She hands him the bottle of water, shushes him to be quiet.

"Like I was saying, as a certified mechanic I strongly advise against it," says Anthony. "My suggestion is that you spend the night here, get a hotel room. There's several near here, and they are all reasonable. Walter over here and I can follow you in my truck, and bring your car back, so we can get started before it becomes quitting time for us. Then we'll get you fixed up first thing tomorrow morning, pick you up and bring you back here to settle the bill, and you can be on your way."

"Don't you think the car will be okay for a few more hours? If it can just make it to Albuquerque, I can get it fixed at a better time."

"Well, if you choose to run for it, I can't stop you. But in my professional opinion you'll be making a big mistake. You stopped to consider the fact that you might not get there if your car shorts out completely out on the freeway, or worse—catches fire? Would you rather get stranded in the middle of nowhere?"

Anthony's colleague—Walter, Anthony called him earlier—a tallish man several years younger, stockily built and ill-at-ease in his uniform, walks up and stands a few feet behind Anthony, taking in the scene.

"Look, we ain't bad people," Anthony says. "We take care of our guests with the best of them. Real Texas hospitality, we got it here."

Zuleikha feels a complete mistress of the situation. She can't decide whether Anthony's suggestion and advice stems from a genuine assessment of what ails her car and a sincere concern about the safety of its passengers, or if there lurks behind them a double-dealing deceitfulness, the insinuation of something lurid or sinister. What was that saying?—the heart sees what the eyes can't—or something like that, Zuleikha thinks, but what about when the heart can't ascertain what the eyes see and the ears hear?

She feels very light, as if lifted off her feet, faced with this choice about whether or not to accept this stranger at his word. Questions sprout in her heart in the manner of wanton weeds, like what's the definition of a stranger, for example, and how do you go about assigning value to his word? If a man you're bound to by law becomes a stranger after six years of knowing him, can anyone else not be? Is strangeness an anodyne or an antidote?

Sentiments flit about her heart like grotesque little insects. She had thought herself self-possessed, changed and strong. Fleeting dreams of a fanciful future were spiriting her onward. And just until a little while ago she had, for the first time in a long while, felt a flash of the joy of abandoning herself to the fantasy that this strange land was a place through which she could glide lightly afoot.

"I'd like you to pull the car outside, please."

"Listen," Anthony begins, when on an impulse she takes her purse off her shoulder and places it on the small corner counter, reaching inside it as if for a weapon or pepper-spray, keeping her hand in there.

"Wow, are you nuts?" Anthony claims, taking a step back. "No need to make a scene...I'm just trying to do my job here, understand?"

"I'd like you to pull the car outside, please," she

repeats, startled, more than anything else, at the strange shrillness of her own voice.

Anthony calls out, "Walter."

Walter mutters something under his breath, gets in her car, and starts it.

"How much do I owe you?" she asks.

"You are nuts," Anthony declares, shaking his head with disgust. "I just want you to know that I ain't responsible for nothin' if your car blows up between here and Albuquerque."

She waits for Walter to get out of her car and step away, then hustles Wasim into the backseat.

Twenty miles later they are in New Mexico. In the rear, Wasim has finally fallen asleep. After another hour of driving across the barren landscape, low hills take shape far away in the left. In the dwindling light of the day, she sees on a sign that Navajo country is not far ahead. The heretofore erect spine of the highway finally begins to hunch over gently to the right, and ominously dark clouds appear in the distance. Brilliant lashes of light tear through them. She catches herself humming in the absence of music from the radio. It strikes her that unlike in the past, approaching thunderstorms no longer fill her with disquietude. She allows herself a smile, continues to drive toward that legion of lightning.

: ACKNOWLEDGMENTS :

I would like to thank the following:

My dear professors at PSU, for all their help, advice, and support—Leni Zumas, Dr. A. B. Paulson, Karin Magaldi, Susan Kirtley, Dan DeWeese, and Deborah Arthur

The following poets and writers for their fellowship, encouragement, and critical feedback on the manuscript: Nancy Taylor, Andrew Mitin, Sean Hennessey, Lily Brooks-Dalton

Sam Leineweber, Deputy District Attorney, Multnomah County, Oregon, Ken Koonce, Director, Legal Action Works Center, Texas, Jay Burke, Multnomah County Department of Community Justice (Domestic Violence Unit), and Michael Crowder, PLLC, Texas, for their selfless help with my research

My publisher Nick Courtright, editor Kyle McCord, and Cammie Finch from Atmosphere Press; Jessica Glenn, Bryn Kristi, and Hannah Richards from Mindbuck Media

Brittany and Becca, whom I love and care for deeply

My mother, and Sonja (my other mother), for their love and for showing me how to lose without losing oneself

Bella, because of whom, everything—including writing—takes me 2.71828 times longer than it should, but without whom, I'd have never found the love and inspiration to complete this book

I would also like to thank Kazim Ali for the excerpt from "Rouen" from *The Far Mosque*. Copyright © 2005 by Kazim Ali. Reprinted with the permission of The Permissions Company, LLC on behalf of Alice James Books, *www.alicejames.org*

: ABOUT ATMOSPHERE PRESS :

Atmosphere Press is an independent, full-service publisher for excellent books in all genres and for all audiences. Learn more about what we do at atmospherepress.com.

We encourage you to check out some of Atmosphere's latest releases, which are available at Amazon.com and via order from your local bookstore:

Itsuki, a novel by Zach MacDonald

A Surprising Measure of Subliminal Sadness, short stories by Sue Powers

Saint Lazarus Day, short stories by R. Conrad Speer

My Father's Eyes, a novel by Michael Osborne

The Lower Canyons, a novel by John Manuel

Shiftless, a novel by Anthony C. Murphy

The Escapist, a novel by Karahn Washington

Gerbert's Book, a novel by Bob Mustin

Tree One, a novel by Fred Caron

Connie Undone, a novel by Kristine Brown

A Cage Called Freedom, a novel by Paul P.S. Berg

Shining in Infinity, a novel by Charles McIntyre

Buildings Without Murders, a novel by Dan Gutstein

: ABOUT THE AUTHOR :

Suman Mallick received his
Master of Fine Arts from
Portland State University,
where he also taught English
and Creative Writing. He is the
Assistant Managing Editor of
the literary magazine *Under
the Gum Tree*. Suman makes

his home in Texas with his beloved daughter and dog, and
his online home at *www.sumanmallick.com*. He may also
be found on Twitter *@smallick71* and on Instagram
@smallick71

CPSIA information can be obtained
at www.ICGtesting.com
Printed in the USA
FSHW011521161020
74818FS